THE DIVINING THREAD

THE DIVINING THREAD

Anjum N. Choudhury

HarperCollins *Publishers* India

First published in India by HarperCollins *Publishers* 2022
4th Floor, Tower A, Building No. 10, Phase II, DLF Cyber City,
Gurugram, Haryana – 122002
www.harpercollins.co.in

2 4 6 8 10 9 7 5 3 1

P-ISBN: 978-93-5629-343-4
E-ISBN: 978-93-5629-344-1

This is a work of fiction and all characters and incidents described in this book are the product of the author's imagination. Any resemblance to actual persons, living or dead, is entirely coincidental.

Typeset in 12/17 Galliard BT at
Manipal Technologies Limited, Manipal

Cover design © Vishnu M. Nair

Printed and bound at
Thomson Press (India) Ltd.

To Ammu and Abbu,
who let me chase my foolish dream
of becoming a writer.

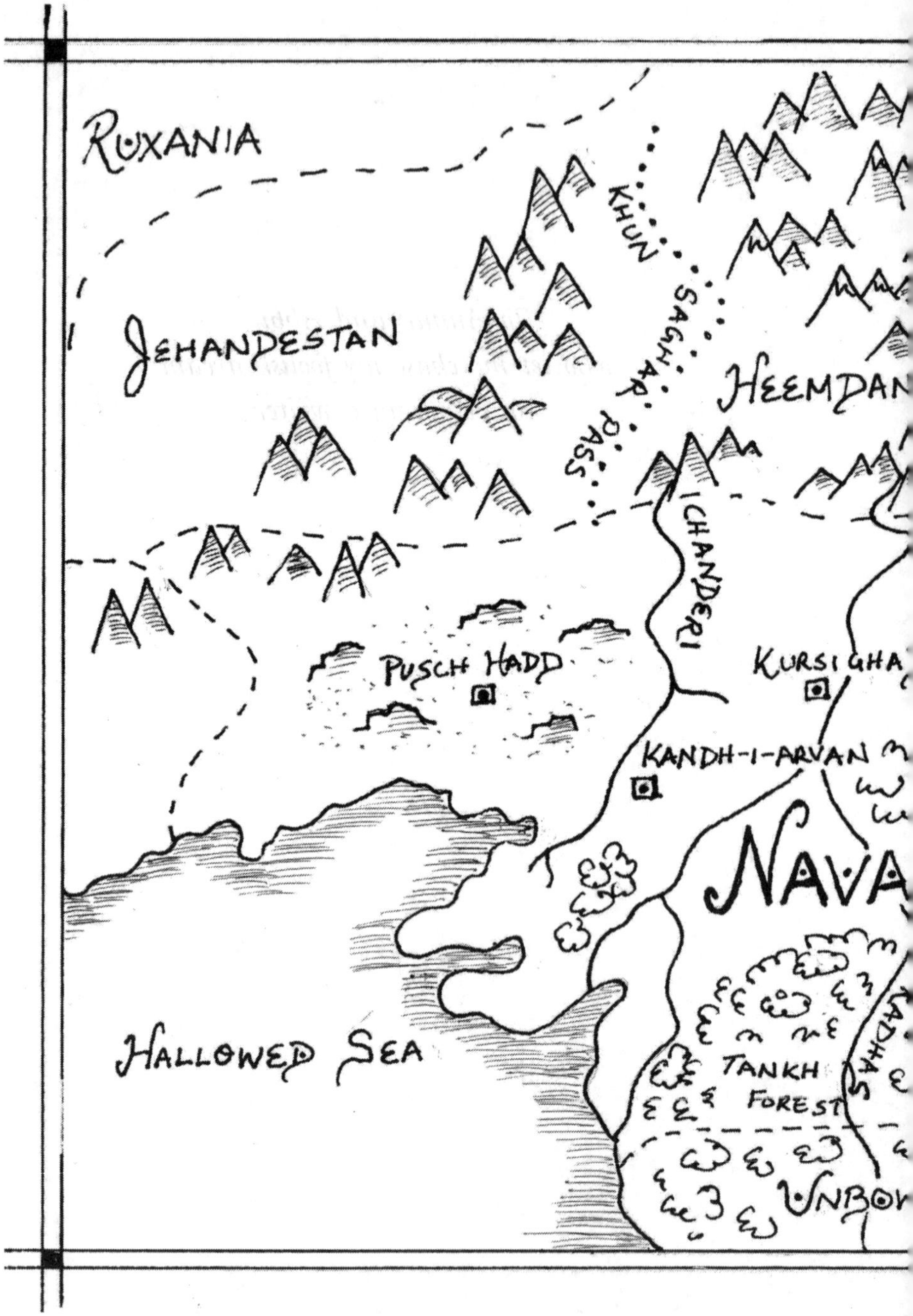
RUXANIA
JEHANDESTAN
KHUN SAGHAR PASS
CHANDERI
PUSCH HADD
KANDH-I-ARVAN
HALLOWED SEA
TANKH FOREST
KADHAS

N
KINGHO
BARWASI
CHO MU MAN PASS
DEWARIA
JIVASPURN
SHANDRABAD
RESHUMNAGAR
BAY OF PLENTY
KINGDOMS

ONE

The bride stared out of her palanquin, transfixed by the village girl's ghagra. The layered skirt cascaded down the girl's bony hips like a spacious tent, yet allowed her to move in unencumbered strides, buoyant in the soft breeze, impervious to all injury from the jungle floor.

Vignettes adorned the ghagra's body, briefly appearing then disappearing somewhere in its many folds. Figures shifted and skipped from one spot to another with every one of its wearer's steps. They told a story, the bride was sure of it. It may have even been one she knew. But the artistry in its telling, and the wonder it promised, tugged at the purest, most vulnerable cord of her heart.

Zarene wished her own wedding finery was half as unique. Clothes fascinated her beyond reason. Though she always concocted new colour schemes, patterns, and outlandish new cuts, she lacked the skill to create much on her own. The rigours of her education and her commitments to her father's estate of Mani Kot left her with precious little time to refine her craft. Whatever time she did have, she spent trying to share her ideas with real artisans.

Tailor masters, weavers, dyers, embroiderers, fabric merchants—they considered her little more than another fanciful patron with a large purse. They flocked to her when news of her betrothal to Prince Naksh Manandha was made public, promising her the finest wedding garb Navaarat would ever know.

The saree she commissioned *was* gorgeous. The purest red silk with intricate flora and fauna was woven in with pure, plied gold. She received a set of gold earrings, a choker, and bracelets fashioned as butterflies from the royal household. Her father had passed on her late mother's gold cummerbund, which was adorned with rubies as large as pigeon eggs.

Beautiful, but heavy and constricting.

Sitting upright, with her legs locked straight before her, Zarene dared not fidget for fear of crumpling her saree. The strain of it sent sweat trickling down her neck and dampened her underarms. She drew deep, faltering breaths, telling herself it would become easier once they reached the embankment. The river winds were sure to cool her down once they boarded the barge to the palace. She tried her best not to worry about the horrible odour of dried sweat on silk, or about how much more she was going to sweat during the ceremony. Pajcathi rituals were notoriously long and theatrical. Marrying a Khalaqan would definitely have been simpler. But a Pajcathi prince was what destiny had planned for her, so she tried, not for the first time, to brace herself for the drawn-out rituals, the heat, the incense—everything. The girl's ghagra was a welcome distraction from her worries. Its gentle sway calmed her frenzied heart, made it easier to breathe. She could have watched the images flickering about its body for days.

The barge would take Zarene's bridal procession up Jivasparn River to the Shandrabad Fort, where she would be married to Naksh on the raja's marble deck. Privy to her rare but potent bouts of disquietude, her father had thought it best she take the less trodden path to the fort, away from the scrutiny of throngs of revellers. Meanwhile, he and his men took a decoy procession through the city of Shandrabad. Dai Ma, her childhood nursemaid, called herself a widow, even though her husband may very well have been alive. Her presence at the wedding would've been deemed inauspicious by the raja's household. Zarene had objected to such superstitions with a passion and would have demanded Naksh to entreat his household had Dai Ma not stopped her.

'You're going to be a princess soon,' Dai Ma had said, stern but affectionate. 'Your heart's desires will rarely be sated from hereon. Duty is to be your only purpose. The sooner you accept that, the lighter your heart will be.'

The girl in the ghagra turned into a narrow dirt path heading deeper into the jungle. Zarene held her breath as the shadows from the trees slowly swallowed the ghagra from view.

'Stop the palanquin!' Zarene called.

Confused murmurs rippled through the procession. The palanquin jerked to a halt. Zarene stuck her head out and pointed. 'Call that girl over here.'

A bemused guard trotted after the girl and fetched her. Her orna, the length of fabric clumsily draped over her chest, hummed in greeting. Zarene's breath caught in her throat.

'Your dress is very unusual,' Zarene said without preamble. Her observations narrowed in on the orna—a thin film of white muslin. Deft, minuscule inscriptions stroked the thread's weft. Zarene heard them—a flurry of voices in her ear, leaving her disoriented yet exhilarated. 'Where did you come by it?'

'I hatched it from an egg,' the girl replied.

Zarene might have laughed if she hadn't been pressed for time. 'Well, you can either bring me the bird who laid it, or you can tell me the truth. I presume you know who I'm going to be after today, what I can do to those who lie to me.'

'I'm not lying,' the girl said, drawing her shoulders back. 'A wayfarer gave me an egg, and I hatched it.'

Tearing her eyes off the garment, Zarene scrutinized its wearer. She was built like a gazelle, wiry and rickety-limbed, perhaps a year or two younger than herself. Her hair, a tawny black from a poor diet and too much time in the sun, was parted into two neat plaits, and her emerald eyes were draped by thick, long lashes.

Zarene ignored her handmaids' appeals to hasten. She beckoned the girl closer and reached for the ghagra. It was like one of her imagined designs had come to life. Four sheer layers of silk. The patterns woven into and embroidered on each layer were fragmented, but together, they looked sublime.

A prickly twinge slipped under Zarene's betrothal ring, twined around it, and sent a paralyzing shock up her arm. She snatched her hand away.

'There's something ... peculiar about it ... something unnatural.'

The girl held her gaze, unaffected. 'Maybe.'

'Zarene Bibi,' a handmaid implored. 'The hour is late.'

Nodding, Zarene wrung feeling back to her hand and pulled out a purse full of silver and gold daulatis she had brought to distribute after the ceremony. 'There's enough here to feed your family for a year. Perhaps more. I'll let you have it in exchange for the ensemble. One of my handmaids will give you a replacement.'

'But I don't need your money.'

'Then—' The wheels spun in Zarene's head. When she spoke, she could not quite believe her own words. 'Take my saree, then. The silk is from worms bred just for the occasion, the gold woven in is pure, and it's been made by three of the greatest masters living today.'

The girl's eyes widened till her lashes touched her brows. 'You'd give up your wedding saree for a village girl's rags?'

Your heart's desires will rarely be sated from hereon.

Well, Zarene would have this last desire fulfilled. Hands growing moist, she repeated, 'My garb for yours.'

The girl's lips pressed into an obstinate line. 'No.'

'I'll return it once I've learnt its make, I promise.'

'But I must wear it today.'

'For the wedding festivities, I understand. And I'm offering you *my* saree in exchange.'

'No.'

Zarene clenched her fists. 'And why, may I ask, isn't the future princess's wedding garb good enough for you?'

The girl remained stoic in her fearlessness. 'I need it to stop the prince from marrying you.'

The tide of gasps crashing over her procession assured Zarene she hadn't misheard.

A guard broke formation and grabbed the girl by her plaits. 'Think you're funny, do you? Bibi, this one's in need of a good flogging to know her place.'

The girl resisted the guard's every pull, her feral green glower unflinching.

'Let her go,' Zarene ordered, incensed by the girl's disrespect. Against her handmaids' protests, she hiked up her saree, climbed out of the palanquin and drew herself up to her full height. She was of a sturdy build, wide-shouldered and hipped, and taller than most women in Shandrabad. Her nose, which always gleamed with a thin sheen of oil, was blunt like a button; her jaw, though feminine and round, was too wide for the rest of her face. She was neither beauty nor beast, but she knew she was capable of both allure and intimidation with the right gaze in her plain black eyes.

'I can understand the value this dress must have to you. I can feel it. But'—Zarene let her words hang in the air—'that doesn't excuse what you just said. Now, either I have my guards drag you to prison and flogged for conspiring against the crown, or you let me study the garment and agree to being escorted home.'

'Fine,' the girl replied, unfazed by Zarene's threat. 'Study it, if that's what you want.'

'Good,' Zarene said, relieved. She picked a handmaid about the same size as the girl, and called her forth. 'Go find someplace to exchange clothes.'

'But I didn't agree to hand them over to you,' the girl said.

'You *just* said ...'

'I said you could study it. And you will do it here. Now.'

'Need I remind you of my station?' Zarene asked through gritted teeth. 'What I am capable of?'

'What are you capable of?' the girl shot back. 'Will you have your guards strip me by force?'

No, Zarene would not. The sensible part of her appealed to accept defeat. There was no time to negotiate further. Dai Ma was right. The sooner she accepted duty as her life's purpose, the easier her choices would be.

The ghagra was a dream come to life, though. How could she just walk away? Something in her snapped. What if this was her last chance to do something she actually cared about?

To her retinue's dismay, she ordered a handmaid to hold her saree's train off the mud. The bowl of turmeric brought to endow the newlyweds with marital harmony was brought out for ink. A bearer's white turban was removed from his head for parchment. A feather from a peahen roaming the vicinity was plucked, its tip shaved to make a quill. For measuring implements, Zarene unfastened her mother's cummerbund from her waist.

She sketched the garment with deft flourishes, noting measurements of her own invention ('betwixt two pigeon-egg rubies, no, make that two-and-a-third pigeon-egg rubies') beside them. She scribbled down words she thought described the feel of the fabric, tested its freefall, and squinted hard to count its threads. She tried to identify the plying method applied to the thread, the exact pattern in which it had been loomed. Most of it was conjecture. It didn't seem impossible to replicate, though. Not with enough trial and error.

The weight of her tardiness loomed heavy over her. A rough study of the orna and ghagra should have sufficed, but the orna's indistinct appeals and the ghagra's lively panels riled her into staying put. She felt like a child in the nursery, cheated out of one last story before the candles were snuffed out.

One of the ghagra's panels depicted a bridal procession, much like her own. A fairly common scene in Navaarati art, this didn't interest her. The figure of a plum giantess, however—spilling over several panels, commanding the devotion of common folk prostrated before her—was another matter. Zarene had never encountered anything like it. The giantess was not like the giants in Dai Ma's nursery tales: boorish, hulking men with wide, lecherous eyes, pointed teeth, and salivating tongues hanging from slack mouths. The giantess wore her height with a courtesan's poise, and she pressed a lotus to her chest to assure her devotees she came in peace.

Her moon-shaped face framed a serene mien, but she could not have been all that content, for the next panel showed her tearing herself apart into twelve smaller women. One of them donned a weatherworn cloak and disappeared into a hollowed tree with a bundle of her belongings. She re-emerged and came upon a crying maiden, to whom she offered her bundle.

Zarene drew a prolonged breath as her eyes raked over the expanse of the ghagra's generous diameter. How many panels were there? How much time did she need to absorb everything? Where did it all begin?

None of it mattered. She had to let go. Immediately. But—

Her hand rebelled against her better judgement, and she started making simplified copies of the panels.

The distant harrying of her servants shot tremors through her writing hand. She continued.

Her heart beat faster with every passing moment, draining all earthly sound from her ears, quickening till she heard nothing but thunder. She had immersed herself so deep into the ghagra's lore that she could not differentiate between her own panic and approaching hoof beats. It was the frightened squirms and collective retreat of her servants that finally pulled her out of her trance.

Flanked by red-liveried guards, Zarene's betrothed slowed to a trot and dismounted from his steed. His white dhoti hung low around his waist, and an embroidered white shawl with thin gold borders was draped over his bare torso. He was a brawny man who led with his chest. There was a time in his youth when his looks were considered feminine, but the deep lines of worry brought on by age and responsibility had since given him a distinguished ruggedness. His hooked nose rose from a deep furrow between his brows, and his forehead stretched up high. A few black curls sprang free from his meticulously slicked mane.

'Stand aside,' he ordered everyone who was not Zarene.

The servants distanced themselves some more. Brimming with anticipation, the village girl attempted to stand her ground but reconsidered upon seeing the rise and fall of his powerful chest.

He strode over to Zarene, head bowed to meet her eyes. 'Are you hurt? We thought you'd been attacked by bandits.'

The tenderness with which he spoke subdued the tension mounting inside Zarene. Theirs was not a love match, but they'd built a bond of trust during their long betrothal. A bond she'd just thrown to the wind because of her wild impulses.

'I'm …' Zarene gulped. 'I'm fine.'

She had to be honest with him. That was what marriages were built of—honesty. The acceptance of one another's flaws. But the shame of admitting to such recklessness, that too on her wedding day, kept her from saying anything.

'Zarene, you were expected at the palace near three hours ago.' In a blink, concern morphed into anger. 'I hope you have a good explanation for disrespecting me and my family like this.'

Zarene looked down at her turmeric-blotted hands.

'Answer me!'

'My prince …' Zarene gathered her wits. 'This girl here has on her a piece of extraordinary craftsmanship. Really one of a kind. I've never seen anything like it.'

Comprehension, however mistaken, flickered across Naksh's features. His nose twitched in disgust. 'Goddesses take me,' he hissed. The pregnant pause that followed was punishment enough, but he continued. 'I can't believe … I thought your obsession with clothes was the same as any woman's. I'd dismissed it as the harmless fancies of an idle mind. Your father and I arranged for you to have the finest artisans at your disposal for today, gave you the finest jewellery all of Navaarat had to offer. Yet, it seems none of that was enough for you. It seems nothing will ever be enough for you.'

'Naksh, it's not like that.'

He silenced her with a raised palm. 'I will not risk having a shallow woman like you for a wife.'

Zarene choked on an incredulous gasp. Angry tears stung her eyes. 'I am not—'

'You are,' Naksh cut her off. 'You have no sense of duty, and your priorities are a disgrace. I should've seen you and your father for the fickle foreigners that you are. I should've known better than to presume the spoiled brat born of a merchant with no name could possess the virtues to rule a kingdom.'

Shaking her head, Zarene searched his eyes. He couldn't have meant that.

As though accepting a challenge, Naksh pivoted to face the girl. 'You, girl, did the sahiba not offer you money for your dress?'

'She did, Your Highness,' the girl replied. Unable to bear the force of his gaze, she trained hers on the ground.

'And? It was not enough?'

'I didn't accept it, Your Highness, so I don't know.'

'Why not?'

'Because it was meant for the people of Shandrabad, Your Highness. To bring glory to your name.' She arched a brow at Zarene. 'It would've been disrespectful of me to take it all for myself.'

Naksh rolled his shoulders back. He clenched his fists and bowed his head in a slight nod, as if to convince himself of something. 'And what is your name?'

'M-my name?' The girl's head snapped up. The razor-sharp confidence she had worn just moments ago seemed a trick of the light. 'My name … Your Highness, I'm just Tumpa.'

'Tumpa. Good,' Naksh replied gruffly. 'Then, with your permission, I will take you as my wife. Are you amiable?'

The world around Zarene swirled out of focus. Her feet remained planted on the ground, but her spirit drifted away. She stared, dumbstruck, as her destined prince hoisted up the mocking ghagra and orna on to his horse, and rode off. Wails of horror pummelled the invisible shield she raised around her. All sense of time and place eluded her. She allowed her servants to lay their hands on her and load her back into the palanquin.

She would be seeing Dai Ma sooner than she had expected.

TWO

How could this happen?

It was the question on everyone's lips when the wedding procession returned to Mani Kot, most of all on the lips of Zarene's father.

'How could this happen?' he muttered over and over again, pacing the length of his sprawling pillared study hall. 'What went wrong?'

Things rarely went so wrong for Rumahn Maimoon. Hailing from the western mountains of Jehandestan, he had come to Navaarat a penniless young man, bent on trying his luck in the land's sophisticated trade lines. He singlehandedly saved a village from being pillaged and scorched by Sultan Jansher's brothers, and won the hand of Zarene's mother in marriage as a reward. Sultan Jansher, then a young prince battling brothers and dissenting nobles for the throne, enlisted Rumahn as a friend and an advisor. Rumahn's prudence and cunning won Jansher his divine seat in Kursighad, and Jansher's generous gratitude equipped Rumahn with the security and funds to create an empire of his own.

He established footholds in every major trade route; dealt in essentials such as salt, grains, tea, spices, cotton and livestock; and earned the trust and loyalty of craftspeople and miners from areas rich in precious stones and building materials. He maintained peace between cities; ensured ministers enforced laws that kept merchants safe, negotiated duties on wares as needed, and advised Sultan Jansher to adjust tributes from the nine provinces to reflect their yearly yields. His insistence also compelled Sultan Jansher to fortify the northwestern border of Navaarat against northern raiders and assign armed escorts to caravans crossing the Khun Saghar Pass to Jehandestan.

Though Navaarat prospered from her father's foresight, Sultan Jansher's court remained sceptical of his true intent because of his Jehand origins, and the people of their adopted home province, Shandrabad, distrusted him for his Khalaqan beliefs. Zarene was barely twelve when demands of her marriage to a Pajcathi man began. Names of low-ranking courtiers three times her age and drunken princes seeking to replenish their incomes with her dowry were proposed. Her father rejected them all until her sixteenth year, when the Raja of Shandrabad himself requested her hand for the crown prince. Naksh was young and dutiful, and in the three years he and Zarene were betrothed, he had seemed of sound mind.

Zarene sighed as she leant against a table stacked to the heavens with leather ledgers and rolls of parchment. She watched her father loop around the chamber's pillars as his thoughts flitted from one conspiracy to the next: this was the ploy of one of his rivals, of Zarene's dejected suitors or even those jealous women who called themselves her friends. They must have tricked her, drugged her into having hallucinations.

Hugging herself, Zarene slipped into a daze. She thought of Naksh, what he was to her now. The hushed, scandalized voices from the procession thrummed in her ear. There were no tears. Just incomprehension and disbelief. A part of her had already accepted that her life was as good as ruined.

Her vision blurred as it tracked her father's movements. All she saw in sharp relief was the way the starched stole over his shoulder flapped against his ivory white panjabi. All she could think of was how clumsy and unwieldy it seemed, compared to the girl—now princess—Tumpa's ensemble.

She thought back to those nerve-wracking hours in the jungle, not to dwell on how she could have defended her reputation to Naksh, but to feel the brush of the ghagra's fabric against her fingers again, and to drown herself in the orna's droning hum.

'They say a witch haunts that jungle,' her father muttered. 'But how should I have known to put stock in such rumours? Creator take me, can it be?'

Zarene snapped out of her reverie.

'Yes, yes.' Her father nodded to himself. His steps quickened, and he grew more unaware of where he was headed. 'It can't be anything but a witch! But why would she curse you? If it's money she wants—it doesn't matter. I'll have the jungle scoured for her.'

'Abba,' Zarene called her father softly.

'And when they find her, I'll have her tongue for cursing my daughter!'

'Abba, I wasn't cursed.'

His sandals scuffed the marble floor as he came to a halt. Tears stung Zarene's eyes. She had never seen him so crestfallen. So vulnerable.

'I wasn't cursed,' she repeated, her voice thick with a repressed sob. 'It was my fault. I should've just done what was expected of me, but I … Abba, I am so sorry. There was no witch. Please don't send your men into the jungle.'

Her father's face twisted in an attempt to conceal his misery. He was a homely looking man, his features round and blunt. The crown of his head was sprinkled with sparse, fine hair. His beard ran a little thicker but still resembled a frayed tassel clinging to a well-worn carpet by its last thread. His unimposing frame made him amiable. The rarity of his smiles made him formidable. Only Zarene knew the swirl of grey in his eyes to be the window into his true feelings. And now he was trying to draw a veil over them to ward her off.

Averting his gaze from her, he wrinkled his nose as though he had caught a whiff of a foul stench.

Her wedding finery … she was still in it. In her rush to give her father a truthful account of what had happened, she had forgotten all about it. The discomfort came flooding back now. Her blouse was soaked through, its silk stuck to her skin.

Her neck was stiff from carrying the weight of her earrings and necklace, and the delicate spot at her tailbone sent dull pulses of pain rippling up her back.

Her father turned his back to her. 'Ah, Creator,' he sighed into the air, miserably. 'I've failed her. How I've failed her.'

Zarene reached out to comfort him but stopped short of touching him. This was her doing. Hot tears streamed down her face to her neck, where they pooled against her choker. With trembling fingers, she searched for the clasp on her mother's cummerbund and undid it.

'Forgive me,' she mumbled under her breath, draping it—rubies shining bright with fury—over a tower of ledgers and withdrawing to her chambers.

❉

'How could this happen?'

The question was terser coming from Dai Ma. She was in the process of snipping the threads fastening the bridal headpieces to Zarene's hair: first the diamond and gold tikli that sat along her middle parting; then the jhapta of stringed pink pearls, emeralds and linked gold draped over her left temple.

Seated before the mirror over her dresser, Zarene surrendered to her nursemaid's sharp tugs as she pulled the ornamental pins from her braid and fished out the grooved bone-pins that held her fine, temperamental tresses in place. Recoiling at the sight of her own haggard reflection, Zarene shifted her focus to Dai Ma's livid reflection instead.

Zarene always wished she had been Dai Ma's real daughter, for she would have been a good deal prettier if she had. Dai Ma was fine-boned, with impeccable, even-toned skin that glowed a wheat gold and large, ever-so-slightly slanted, almond-shaped eyes that were canopied by thick, angular brows. Her habit of only wearing shades of grey accentuated her picturesque beauty. *The deceit of contrasts*, Zarene called it—plain garments to heighten attractive features, ornate ones to dull plainness.

Had I been Dai Ma's daughter, I would've never cared for pretty clothes. And I would've never ended up where I am today.

Shame dug its claws in her. Dai Ma had weathered things, terrible things, that Zarene could never comprehend. Zarene knew that before coming to work at Mani Kot as her wet nurse, Dai Ma had been married for ten years. She had survived four near-fatal miscarriages and birthed three healthy daughters, who were just as beautiful as she was. After giving birth to her fourth, a stillborn boy, her husband cast her and the girls out and married again. Dai Ma came to Mani Kot with Kalindi, Pakhi and Rahi after that. The girls had been clothed, fed and educated alongside Zarene, and were now married to good men from good households. But they'd never known a father's love as Zarene had, even though they were more deserving of it.

Tearing her gaze from Dai Ma's reflection, Zarene looked at the heap of jewellery lying on her dresser. Naksh had been right. She *was* a spoiled brat. A long-drawn sigh of defeat deflated her chest.

Dai Ma freed Zarene's wavy black hair from its braid with practised fingers, then rolled it into a bun that she pinned to the crown of her head. 'That's that, then,' she sighed, weariness replacing the terse slant of her mouth. 'Come, on your feet now. You've been in that saree long enough.'

Zarene pivoted, round and round and round, until she was unspooled from the garment. Once she had pulled her night kaftan over her head, Dai Ma sat her back down at the dresser with a vial of coconut oil to remove the kohl from her eyes, the carmine from her lips and the betel juice from her cheeks.

She was slow to smear the oil over her face. Halfway through wiping the kohl from one eye, she stopped. She didn't want to remove the colour from her face. Doing so meant she definitely wasn't getting married that day. It meant she'd truly ruined her future over a peasant girl's clothes.

'How could this happen?' Zarene asked.

Dai Ma's mouth opened, a slew of reprimands on the tip of her tongue. Her chest heaved with a despairing sigh. She sat down beside Zarene, took the cloth from her rigid fingers, and wiped the rest of her face clean.

'What's done is done,' she said. 'I won't have you making yourself sick over this, do you hear?'

'But—'

It was a knock at the door, not Dai Ma, that interrupted her.

'Enter,' Dai Ma called.

The door opened a crack to let through one of Zarene's handmaids. She shut the door quickly to conceal the throng of inquisitive servants gathered outside. Resting in her hands was an ornate silver chest. From her gait under its weight, Zarene gathered it was empty.

'It arrived from the prince's palace, Bibi.'

'He's sent for the jewellery,' Dai Ma hissed. 'The nerve of that son of a swine. As uncouth as he is unfaithful.'

'It doesn't matter, Ma. The sooner I sever ties with him, the better.'

Zarene didn't care that her hands were still coated in oil. She scooped the pile of gold on the dresser and held it out to the maid. 'Here, take it.'

'But the rider has already left, Bibi,' the girl said. She patted the box with care. 'He said the prince means for you to have this.'

Exchanging a look with Dai Ma, Zarene sprang to her feet. She hastily wiped her hands clean and traced the chest's carved ridges before taking it from the girl and setting it down on her bed. Lifting the lid by its catch, she froze.

'Leave us,' Dai Ma ordered the girl.

The handmaid attempted a peek into the box, but was cowed by Dai Ma's warning glare. Head bowed, she retreated. The rustle of speculation outside rose for a beat before she clicked the heavy door shut.

Dai Ma peered over Zarene's shoulder. 'What's the meaning of this?'

The phantom twinge returned to Zarene's ring finger, which was now bare. Soft currents of energy streamed through her fingers and up her arms as her hands hovered over two halves of an eggshell. Tumpa's clothes from the jungle lay underneath. It felt less hostile this time. The jumbled song emanating from the orna prodded her to let it seep deeper and bind itself to her very being.

'Don't!' Dai Ma stayed her hands. 'He means to humiliate you. Have it returned at once.'

'It doesn't matter,' Zarene said, her voice hoarse. It really didn't, for she was already doomed to live the rest of her life with this humiliation. The dress was her only consolation. And it belonged to her now.

Had the day not shaken her to her core, she might have actually relished this.

Put together, the eggshell halves, though brittle as eggshells ought to be, formed an egg the size of a melon. It was too large to come from any bird. The ghagra and orna fit inside them with ease, confirming they had indeed been hatched, just as the girl had said.

It was all a trick, of course. To convince Zarene she was mad. She knew a number of sweet-makers who made such shells with sugar and colouring. She broke off a bit of the shell and bit into it. Tasteless with a sandy crunch, like all eggshells. She spat it out. No matter. She still knew she was right.

A silent vow took shape as she tipped the garment out of the shells and splayed it across her bed. With all the time in the world to do as she pleased now, she was going to learn all the dress's secrets. And when she did, she was going to make more of them. And after every woman in Shandrabad, noble and common alike, had enjoyed the graceful cuts of her work, she was going to send a set to Naksh. He could mock her all he wanted now. She was going to prove him wrong.

Climbing into the bed, she patted the space across from her for Dai Ma to join her. The expanse of the ghagra's width took up most of the bed. Some of it spilt off the sides.

'Look at these,' Zarene said, pointing at the panels. 'It's telling a story, see. Only, I don't know it. Do you?'

She ignored the bewildered look on Dai Ma's face and found her place—the giantess' scion offering the crying maid her bundle. Inside it was a spherical object that encased a dress within: an egg.

Zarene's stomach lurched.

The girl donned the dress and came upon a bridal procession. The bride climbed out of her palanquin—

Zarene skimmed over subsequent panels: The prince mounted his steed with the maid in his arms. A group of nobles with upturned noses and pointed fingers cast the once-bride from their company. Face buried in her hands, the once-bride lay on her back, alone. And then—

She disappeared. A cast of unfamiliar characters crowded the panels like cattle—bickering, dancing, making love, killing. Zarene searched the rest of the ghagra, even turned the garment inside out, but found nothing.

Her story had ended. She had nothing to look forward to. Nothing to live for.

The vow she'd made moments earlier evaporated and dread took its place.

How can that be?

A different, quieter voice, asked the same question. How *can* that be?

She was young, privileged, intelligent and—dare she say it? Ambitious. She could have a dozen things to live for if she wanted.

But first, she had to free herself from the offending object that brought her here.

'Scissors,' she muttered, climbing off the bed. 'Give me my scissors.'

Dai Ma did not move. 'Zarene, what on earth are you ... will you just explain wha—'

Zarene grabbed the scissors Dai Ma had used to undo her hair. Snipping the air, she took one last look at the ghagra and orna before lowering the blades and shredding them. The suffocating darkness loosened its grasp on her with every *slash* and *zip* of tearing fabric. The foreign sensations coursing through her bloodstream dulled in their vigour, before fading altogether. When there was nothing left except for a heap of scraps and stray threads, Zarene almost moaned in relief.

'Get rid of it,' she ordered Dai Ma. 'Burn it for all I care.'

Dai Ma gaped at her, stunned by what must have seemed like an irreversible descent into madness. She arched a scrutinizing brow at Zarene before concluding that the worst was over. Collecting the scraps of fabric, she headed out.

'Try to get some sleep,' she said over her shoulder. 'It's been a long day.'

Alone, Zarene looked about her empty chambers. Had everything gone as planned, she would have been with Naksh at that moment, consummating their marriage. She let out a shaky breath. Perhaps she was never meant to wed Naksh to begin with.

She slipped into a deep, dreamless sleep. When she woke the next morning, the ghagra and orna hung from the bottom-left post of her bed, fully intact.

The dress remained a fixture in Zarene's life. There was just no getting rid of it.

She tried everything—tearing it, burning it, burying it, submerging it in corrosive concoctions—but it always returned to her the next morning, unharmed, its effect on her no less potent. Word soon spread through the household that Zarene Bibi was in possession of a cursed dress that threatened to drive her mad.

But while all signs pointed to the dress being cursed, Zarene was far from mad. She was the most focused she had ever been, and she held fast to that quiet thread of common sense inside her. Rather than allowing the garment's devious attachment to her faze her, she set about trying to replicate it. She enlisted expert artisans to theorize on the nature of the fabric used, the number of shafts a loom required to achieve such results, and the ensemble's stylistic origins. Being a fair embroiderer herself, she tried replicating the embroidery style on layers of sheer fabric. The end results were decent, but nowhere near as marvellous without the ensemble's woven base.

Her father busied himself as well, assessing the merit of prospective suitors for her—more of the same courtiers, ministers and drunk princes he had turned away since she was twelve. Her answer was always no, no matter how much talk there was in Shandrabad of her madness and, worse, her impending spinsterhood. She would not entertain another man in her life until she had refuted Naksh's claim of her being a spoiled brat.

When the pool of not-even-decent prospects ran dry, her father accepted defeat by taking off for Kursighad to discuss state matters with Sultan Jansher. Zarene suspected 'state matters' had less to do with the past year's drought than with increasing the Manandhas' tribute to the capital in the coming year.

He was proud as he was clever, her father, but only in the outside world. Within the halls of Mani Kot, he didn't have it in him—didn't know how—to argue with women, especially Zarene.

'If only your Amma had been alive,' he sighed, pressing her cheeks, then taking her leave.

The day after he left, an invitation arrived from Shandrabad Fort. It was for a mehfil celebrating Princess Tumpa's first month as a member of the Manandha household.

'You will not go,' Dai Ma snapped. 'I won't stand him shaming you for spectacle.'

'The invitation is addressed to me,' Zarene said, tracing the invitation's ribbed calligraphy. She would have gladly declined if it was her father's name on the scroll, but this was a blatant challenge. 'Naksh won't get the spectacle he wants, but I'm not going to give him the satisfaction of thinking me a coward.'

THREE

The evening of the mehfil, Zarene donned the cursed ghagra and orna despite Dai Ma's repeated entreaties not to. Given how much the ensemble occupied her thoughts at all times, it was a wonder this was the first time she actually put it on. She supposed it was because, contrary to what Naksh said, her interest in it had always been scholarly.

The ensemble felt like a weightless cloud embracing her. At the same time, the weight of its hidden secrets made her knees buckle. She paired the ghagra with white churidar pajamas and a white muslin choli lined with pale silver satin, which was fastened at the back with tasselled ties. Dai Ma stitched the orna to the crown of her head, draped one half over her torso and tucked it into the ghagra's waistband. The other half flowed down her back.

The figure staring back at her from the mirror looked like a clever imitation of her—richer in features, more beautiful. *A deceit of contrasts.*

The belief that she looked like a different person inured her to the barrage of whispers and stares that greeted her when she arrived at the prince's palace in the Shandrabad Fort, carrying an ornate dala packed with gifts. It was against custom for men to converse with unmarried women without chaperones at such gatherings, but even the women—most of whom were acquainted with Zarene—refused to meet her eyes, let alone speak to her.

'Is that it, *the* dress?' a tactless woman whispered loudly.

'Oh, if it is, why, I dare say!'

Zarene's steps faltered. The gifts inside the dala threatened to spill out from underneath the marigold gossamer shrouding it. As though it sensed her self-doubt, the orna kissed her earlobes. Its many whispers conjured a tidal wave in her ears, stoppering them from hearing anything other than its drawn-out moan. Soothed to an extent, Zarene followed the procession of guests to the Nakshan Palace.

The nasal drawl of a duet of shehnai flutes snaked through the air. Soft pads of the tabla, and the gush and tinkle of water rounded out the dignified milieu. The open-air reception court was built inside a vast pool of hip-deep water, which shimmered blue because of the lapis lazuli embedded in its floor. The marble platform at the centre, inlaid with precious stones, was flanked by low, perforated marble enclosures. A bridge branched out from each of the four sides to porches that led to the palace's interior.

On the far side of the court, manned by armed guards, stood a raised dais housing the prince's canopied throne. The women of his household were seated behind him, obscured by a thin screen of rust-pink gauze.

Musicians were stationed at the court's fringes. Around them, water erupted from fountains in the pools, cascading down like diamond waterfalls under the light of the braziers standing behind them. Courtesans awaited their cue on the porch to the right. A tributary of women diverged from the main inflow of guests to take their seats on the screened porch to the left and balconies above it.

Zarene craned her neck for a good look at the guests waiting to be called before Naksh – all men. Shandrabad was one of the few princely cities in Navaarat to practise segregation on stately occasions. A woman's ability to melt into the margins was deemed a sign of good breeding – a talent Zarene, to the muffled gasps of keen bystanders, decided not to exercise as she joined the queue of well-wishers.

Stealing a glance at the women's porch every now and then, Zarene stood her ground. Her knuckles turned pale from gripping the dala too tight.

You can do this, she chanted under her breath. *Do it, and it will be done.*

A mass of orange brocade slid in between her and the guest in front of her. The mouldy stench of ill-dried clothes and body odour startled Zarene into taking a few steps back.

The garish orange qaba coat embellished with an oversized peacock brooch belonged to a man roughly her height. A line of gold rings adorned his ears. His pointed nose and chin were framed by overstuffed, pockmarked cheeks. The turquoise gemstone on his silver ring had purple swirls in it that seemed to move as the stubby finger wearing it came up to scratch his temple. His eyes squeezed together in appraisal of her.

'Maimoona Sahiba, is it not?'

The corner of his mouth, blackened from chewing tobacco, tugged up in what he must have considered a charming smile. Zarene swallowed the bile rising up her throat. There was some comfort in knowing her large dala blocked him from getting too close.

'I was hoping you might be here tonight,' he said, his torso craning over the dala. 'You may not know who I am, but your father and I—'

'Shurram Sahb,' Zarene blurted out. She flashed him a trite smile. 'I know who you are.'

'Ah,' he exhaled, enveloping her in a burst of tobacco reek. 'That's fortunate. Very fortunate.'

Laal Shurram was one of the names vying for her hand that her father vehemently refused, both before and after her broken betrothal. He owned a great many lands in and around Shandrabad but was a notorious spendthrift. His tenants bore the brunt of his lavish ways. Not a month could pass without news of another farmer tenant killing himself for not being able to pay Shurram's exorbitant rent.

'I'm terribly sorry to hear what happened with, well, you know.' He flicked a wrist at the throne. In a low voice, he continued, 'I was just appalled when he showed up with that peasant girl. To think *she* could be a princess in your stead. Just unthinkable!'

'Well, she *is* the princess now,' Zarene said, sounding uninterested. She trained her gaze past him, hinting she wished to be left alone.

'You must not lose hope, Sahiba. Any man, and I do mean *any* man, would be lucky to claim you as his bride. You may not know this, but I had actually offered to take you—'

'*Take* me?'

Shurram waved off her indignation. 'You know what I mean. I expressed my interest to your father, and well … I can understand how a father might be hesitant to rush into things so soon after an affair *so* scandalous, but the key to these things is to strike while the iron is still hot.'

'Actually, I think my father's answer was a definitive no.'

'Well, he was in an emotional state. It's to be expected. But you, Sahiba, are the one marrying in the end, and I think it's only fair you decide. Here'—he pulled on the dala—'why don't I carry this?'

'That won't be necessary.' Zarene's grip tightened. 'Really.'

He went on tugging, drawing attention from the other guests. Rage flared inside Zarene. The whispers in her ear simmered to a boil. A surge of strength swept through her, and she used the dala to shove Shurram into the man in front of them.

Her composure snapped back into place, as though nothing had happened, just as the man turned around and glowered at Shurram.

'Deep in your cups already, are you, Shurram?' the man guffawed heartily enough. He clapped a hand on Shurram's shoulder. 'At least *try* to mind yourself in front of the womenfolk.'

'Forgive me, Bakshan Sahb,' Shurram chuckled apologetically. He scratched his temple with his turquoise-ringed finger. Removing himself from the line of well-wishers, he gave Zarene a curt, narrow-eyed bow. 'I'll remember to keep you in my prayers, Sahiba.'

He sneered at her before turning with a flourish of his qaba. Nonchalantly treading to the musicians by the enclosure, he tossed them a few copper daulatis before crossing over to the porch to flirt with the courtesans.

More curses. Just what Zarene needed.

The rest of the wait passed without incident. Her run-in with Shurram and the ensuing whispers dulled her apprehensions about facing Naksh and Tumpa again. When the master of ceremonies finally called her name, she conducted herself with grace and dignity.

Tumpa's eyes burned an iridescent green through the gauze screen, like those of a cat hunting at night. Her excitement practically singed Zarene's skin as she approached the dais. It did not escape Zarene how Naksh's sisters discreetly held Tumpa still amidst the lofty cushions, and whispered harsh reproaches in her ear.

On the throne, doing his best not to reprimand his wife himself, Naksh shifted uncomfortably, bowing his head in greeting.

'Mothers bless you, Sahiba,' he said, his lips pressed in a stern line. An agitated scuffle behind the screen made him tighten his clutch on the throne's arm. 'You honour me with your presence here tonight.'

The muscles in Zarene's cheeks ached from holding her smile. She set the dala on the viewing stand before him and pulled the shroud off. 'If I may, I would like to present His and Her Highnesses with a few tokens of congratulations: mangoes from the gardens of Mani Kot, a few blocks of Chatulian molasses, a collection of dyes, and a bolt of brocaded silk from the famous Surjalok Chowk at Reshumnagar.'

They were simple gifts—perhaps too simple to offer a prince—but Naksh did not have the chance to look unimpressed.

'Let go of me!' Tumpa's voice cut through the music and conversation. 'I must … I must … she'll listen. She has to … let me—'

She broke free of Naksh's sisters and burst through the screen. Pouncing on Zarene, she flashed her a pleading smile. The dark rings around her eyes made her cheekbones look sharper. Her shimmering green eyes looked even more predatory up close. Hers was not the face of a pampered princess. It was that of a starving urchin, half-crazed from hunger. 'That's my dress,' she whimpered, struggling to stay courteous. 'This … this—'

Naksh directed a low growl at his sisters. His knuckles had gone white with strain.

'It's all well, Your Highnesses,' Zarene assured him. She drew Tumpa aside and embraced her. The girl was taut to the point of snapping. 'Creator bless you, Your Highness. Please accept my heartiest congratulations on what will be a most fruitful marriage.'

She pretended not to notice Tumpa's clutch on the orna as she drew away.

'Give it back,' Tumpa half hissed, half sobbed. 'You've got to give it back.'

'I don't understand.' Zarene tried to pry the orna free. 'This was a gift, Your Highness, and to return a gift—that too from the princess of Shandrabad—is great folly. Surely, someone has briefed you on such etiquette?'

'Please!' Tumpa's nails dug into Zarene's flesh. 'Didi, I beg you. I made a mistake. I thought I'd humiliate you for challenging me, for talking down to me, but I was wrong. I was so, so wrong. I can't, you see … without the dress. Without it, I'm a laughing stock. I hear them whispering terrible things about me day and night, even in my sleep. Please, I can't go on like this. Please, Didi, you've got to give it back!' Her voice grew dark and feral. 'Now! Take it off!'

Clawing Tumpa off of her, Zarene held her at arm's length. 'My apologies, Your Highness, but I think my presence here is ailing you.'

'Shut up, shut up, shut up! Just shut up and do as I say!'

The rumble of conversation in the court petered to a halt. The musicians doubled their efforts to fill the silence, but it was futile. All eyes were on the throne.

Zarene released Tumpa with a slight shove.

On his feet by now, Naksh put himself between the two women. 'Zarene,' he said, his severe features soft and imploring, 'this is all … unforgivably improper. I don't know what—'

'I think I've heard enough for one evening,' she cut him off. 'I hope the presents are to your liking. The night is still young, and your evening may yet be salvaged. I'll take my leave now.'

She didn't wait for a response. The line of waiting guests parted to grant her passage out. The pleats of her ghagra realigned themselves to allow her faster movement. The orna grew heavy on her head and shoulders, protective like chainmail. An odd prickling in her ears heightened all her senses.

Run.

Her steps quickened without question.

'No!' Tumpa cried out from behind. 'Don't just stand there; she's a thief. Grab her! Grab her!'

The distance to the gate seemed to stretch several kos. Tumpa's accusation tailed her, echoing through the porches and turbaned heads she sped past. Guards in red livery wove through the guests and closed in on her. Outstretched arms speared at her. The path ahead and around her shrank.

But nothing touched her.

The threads fastening the orna to her hair sprang free. The swath of white tented over her head and twirled like a courtesan's skirts. It swatted the encroaching mob off their feet, into the air. The stays at the ghagra's waist dug into Zarene's flesh as its hem fluttered into the air, unleashing a vengeful windstorm on the courtyard.

The orna unfurled to its full size and wound around Zarene like a cocoon. She flailed her arms, clawed at the fabric with her nails, pressed her open mouth against it for want of air. But the orna's grip continued to tighten, squeezing the breath out of her until her vision turned blurry and her body collapsed.

❈

She hit weeds and dust. White sunlight scorched her skin. The orna lay strewn, lifeless, beside her. She scrambled to her feet and shielded her eyes. She was on an arid plain. Far from Nakshan Palace or anywhere else in Shandrabad. A cloud of dust—*a sand storm?*—encroached on her from the southeastern horizon. Heart pounding in her ear, she scanned the terrain for shelter, but not a single tree or structure was in sight. The storm surged towards her at breakneck speed. There was no choice but to run.

The heat wore her down, draining the strength from her legs. She was so parched she could hardly breathe. Behind her, the distant rumble of thunder morphed into roars as the storm gained on her. But the heat remained still. *No wind.* Underfoot, rocks and pebbles skipped and shuddered from reverberations pulsing through the ground.

Over her shoulder, through the tall cloud of dust, she made out an undulating shadow. Flashes of white hovered close to the ground, pointed and curved like scimitars. As it sped closer, the shadow split and hardened into distinct figures. Those were not scimitars. They were tusks that were about to skewer her—the tusks of a herd of elephants.

The beasts were upon her before she could so much as blink. Throwing her arms over her head, she hunkered down and waited for the inevitable. For the final crush. But it did not come. They sped past her as though she were a boulder in their path.

A pair of tusks scooped her up as she lowered her arms. Before she could register what was happening, the elephant carrying her sped forth with the rest of the herd. Her scream got lost in the rush of wind whipping her face.

She held on to the tip of the nearest tusk for dear life. A shadow glided over her, dulling the sun's burn. Squinting, Zarene saw the unfurled orna drifting overhead. It sang its usual cacophony of whispers. Only now, Zarene felt their meaning deep in her bones.

There is a song they will not hear, they seemed to say. *Its tune so strange and yet so dear.*

Zarene stared at the orna, perplexed.

As Zarene's carrier hurtled forward, the herd parted. Her eyes stung from the dust and wind, but through the tears, she saw a chasm opening up before them—the deepest, most magnificent stepwell she had ever seen. It drew closer, but her carrier showed no signs of slowing down. Zarene broke into a cold sweat. She backed up against the elephant's trunk, imploring it to stop.

A few strides from the edge, it bucked onto its hind quarters, skidded to a dusty halt, and tossed Zarene into the stepwell's mouth. Down she fell, past several million flights of stairs lining the stepwell's walls. The sheen of water shone below, but it was brown. The water was shallow. Her neck would most definitely snap on impact.

Why? Why me?

A Khalaqan call to prayer—melodic and soothing—sounded somewhere in the distance.

Why am I being punished?

Her arms slack from exhaustion, Zarene shut her eyes, confused and resigned in equal measure.

But the impact never came. She stilled mid-air, just as her nose touched the water's surface. Before she could sigh in relief, something soft snaked around her waist—the orna. Like a pail on a pulley, it drew her up to the stepwell's wall, depositing her on the summit of a pair of steps.

Before her lay a door opening into a dark passage. The orna draped itself over Zarene's chest and imbued her senses with the same words as before.

A strain so strange and yet so dear.

Too tired to resist, wishing for nothing but to return to Mani Kot, Zarene clutched the orna to her heart and stepped through.

She entered a dimly lit, lush grove. The leaves were an unhealthy yellowish green, covered in white, wriggling, writhing needles.

A colossal throne wrought from tree roots rose from the earth. On it sat a giantess, her skin so translucent, Zarene could see her wine-coloured blood pulsing underneath. Her face had no discernable features. Zarene only saw her own face reflected in her clear blood. Enticed by her stillness, Zarene reached out for a feel of the giantess's extraordinary skin. Her hand came up against nothing, but she felt something. Something akin to fine muslin laid over cool marble.

Plump lips materialized on the plum face. The words that spilt out sent a wave of heat through Zarene's veins:

There is a song they will not hear,
A strain so strange and yet so dear.
Savour it and trust it you must,
Steadfast and certain as solitude and dust.
A bard's song sung may ring empty,
Where silence holds the key to aplenty.

Zarene opened her mouth to ask what it meant, but the grove swirled out of focus and disappeared.

❈

She crashed back into her body with a start. Pulling the orna from her face, she found herself back at Naksh's mehfil. The braziers and candles had been snuffed out. Nothing but moonlight bathed Naksh's quiet court, where groaning, half-conscious guests lay strewn across the floor.

Wincing at the ache in her back and rear from crashing into hard marble, Zarene sat up and set about straightening her clothes. A flash of crimson on her ghagra caught her eye. Flattening the spot on the floor, she let out an excited gasp. It was a brand-new panel.

A rough hand yanked her to her feet before she could get a good look. 'Come with me.'

Naksh ignored her protests and dragged her past the confused guests into a private audience chamber inside the palace. He shrank at the withering glare she shot him when he let go. His hands fidgeted at his sides as he tried to collect himself. Zarene had never seen him so rattled.

'What did you do to her?' he asked. 'Why won't she wake?'

Zarene baulked. 'I can't say. Maybe you should take better care of your wife.'

'Zarene, need I remind you that I am prince of—'

'And I came here at *your* invitation, wearing a gift you and *your wife* sent me. Have care before acting the innocent victim.'

'I could have your head for speaking to me like this.'

'Go ahead. I'd love to see how the Manandha dynasty survives a son with a mad wife and Sultan Jansher's wrath.'

'Smite you with the Mothers' blight!' He slammed a nearby pillar. 'This isn't what I wanted. I wanted us to be together, to make a prosperous life, raise Shandrabad to heights my father could never conceive of.'

'And your idea of making that life was to abandon me at the first opportunity that presented itself?'

'It's that wretched dress!' He raked his fingers through his dishevelled curls. 'Believe me, I sensed something wrong with it the moment I set Tumpa on my saddle.'

And you still married her, Zarene wanted to cry.

Naksh's shoulders slumped. 'We were betrothed three years. Our bond was forged in truth.' He drew a prolonged breath. 'You know I'm not a superstitious man, but given everything that's happened, I thought it'd be best to get rid of it. Tumpa wouldn't part with it, so I suggested she gift it to you as'—he couldn't stop himself from grimacing—'a show of magnanimity. I convinced her it was the sort of thing a woman of her station would do.'

'Along with humiliating me. How convenient.'

'What happened today bodes ill for us all. So long as that dress exists, people will say the three of us are cursed. And what if they're right, Zarene? I've made my decision. It has to be destroyed.'

'*You've* made your decision?' Zarene scoffed at his pompousness. 'Well, I'm sorry to have to tell you, but I've tried to destroy it, and it can't be done.'

'Then you haven't tried hard enough,' he barked.

'I've tried *everything*,' Zarene said, her voice thick with venom. 'I can return it, of course. You can try for yourself. Who knows, Tumpa may even regain her sanity if she gets it back.'

'Back to being a simple peasant girl, yes,' Naksh mumbled to himself. He collapsed on a cushioned carpet and buried his face in his hands. 'Mothers take me, what am I going to do?'

Zarene stared at him, resentment wrenching her guts. How she longed to rub salt in his wounds. In her best imitation of Dai Ma, she said, 'We bear the consequences of our actions, be the fruit ripe or rotten. I used to think you were a smart man. Maybe you'll learn from your mistakes.'

When he uncovered his face, there was a far-off look in his eyes. He swallowed hard before just saying, 'Zarene.'

Zarene recognized the expression he wore. It was trust of the most intimate kind. One that could only be painstakingly nurtured over three long years of betrothal. But what good was that now? Any affection she had for him was eclipsed by blind rage. Before she lost all control, she turned on her heel and hurried out to her palanquin.

The rise and dip of her ride, and the low, rhythmic *humma humma hums* chanted by the palanquin's bearers eased the tightness in her chest. When she finally stopped seeing red and managed to unclench her fists, she sought out the new panel on her ghagra. Parting the palanquin's drapes a sliver, she aligned the layers of fabric and studied them in the moonlight.

The crimson embroidery and weave formed a rose garden, not unlike the one her bed-chamber overlooked. Two figures strolled through it. The first she recognized as herself. The second, a child.

FOUR

Plenty of children roamed the grounds of Mani Kot. All the maids, gardeners, cooks, sweepers and errand boys had families who lived on the estate, but none of them, especially children wont to pluck and trample flowers, were allowed in Zarene's private rose garden.

Savour it and trust it you must.

Steadfast as solitude and dust.

Zarene's heart beat for those words, but it eluded her how a child could be the key to understanding the ensemble's make; how it would bring her closer to proving the worth of her pursuits.

Zarene combed through all the residents of Mani Kot, hoping to find the child depicted on the ghagra. She went into the servants' quarters, made trifling conversation with awestruck children, and inquired about where they bought and how they made their clothes. Much as they all tried to tailor their answers to her liking, no one had anything new or useful to tell. Some of the young girls she spoke to shared their own clothes-making and mending tasks with her. Zarene wondered if they'd be interested in apprenticeships under artisans, and if they'd mind her patronage. At least some good would come from all this then.

Meanwhile, the more Zarene tried to riddle out the newly appeared panel's meaning, the more Dai Ma withdrew. An unsettling distance had crept in between them since the night of the mehfil. While she honoured all her obligations to Zarene, she did so irritably, without her usual poise or warmth. She barely spoke to Zarene anymore. When she had no choice but to consult her on estate affairs, her words were terse and her demeanour bereft of all emotion.

Zarene felt guilty, though she was not sure why. More than anything, she felt alone. When Zarene was a child, Dai Ma and her daughters had been her constant companions. After Kalindi, Rahi and Pakhi married and left Mani Kot, it was just her and Dai Ma. Zarene shared everything with her, asked her counsel on every decision she ever made. To now face the unknown without her was terrifying.

With no one to placate her fears and frustrations, Zarene was driven to tears night after night. The halls of Mani Kot seemed too vast, yet the haveli itself seemed to close in around her. Soon she did not have the energy to pull herself out of bed because of the futility of it all. A great invisible slab of marble sat on her chest, crushing the air from her lungs, paralysing her senses. The sunniest of days seemed dark. Not that she could really tell one day from the other anymore; they all seemed to draw out in one cold, never-ending night.

Things could not carry on like this. She couldn't allow herself to become as deranged as Tumpa. The possibility made her shudder, but what was she supposed to do? She needed a glimmer of hope. And she needed her Dai Ma.

When everyone's apathy towards her became unbearable, Zarene decided to summon Kalindi, Rahi and Pakhi back to Mani Kot. A few laughs with them would make everything better. As she sat composing letters to each of the three, she decided to summon their children as well.

And then it occurred to her.

If the child depicted in the new panel was not of Mani Kot, she would need to have more children brought to her.

❈

'We'll host a mela,' Zarene told Dai Ma, giddy with excitement. 'Open the grounds to the children of Shandrabad for seven days. Why, we can send word as far as Shornapur and Chatuliganj.'

They were in the study hall. Zarene pulled out the ledger for the household's finances. She intended to pay for the festivities using the savings from her own allowances, but she knew that might not be enough. Her father usually kept a lump sum set aside for mejbans and other such occasions.

Settling down at one end of the elongated worktable that spanned the length of the hall, Zarene wrote out a list of things that needed to be organized for the occasion.

'Do you think a hundred goats will be enough to feed everyone for a week?' She scribbled a note next to the number. 'We'll have to hire a few vegetarian cooks for the Pajcathis, and a separate kitchen will have to be set up. They'll need to be away from where the children will play of course. And the entertainment will have to be plentiful … not to mention varied. They say children can be fickle creatures.'

'What—'

Zarene's head shot up.

It was the first word Dai Ma had spoken to her all day. The older woman regarded her with a stern set to her mouth, the muscles in her neck taut. For all her efforts to rein in what she felt, she could not hide the quaver in her words. 'When … *if* you do find this child, what do you intend to do?'

'I don't know.' Zarene had never considered *why* the ghagra showed her the child. She supposed the ghagra would tell her what to do next when she'd found him. 'Maybe he'll be in need of a home.'

'And then? What becomes of him when you marry? Will your husband allow you to bring the child with you?'

'If he cannot put up a helpless child, even after he's been paid my dowry, maybe I shouldn't be marrying him.'

'Zarene!' Dai Ma bellowed. Her eyes bulged and nostrils flared. 'Do you have *any* idea of the situation you've put yourself in? Have you learnt nothing of a husband's expectations after what's happened?'

Chewing the inside of her cheeks to keep herself from raising her voice, Zarene returned Dai Ma's glare, stippling parchment with her quill as she did. 'I admit what I did that day was wrong,' she said, tartly. 'But what's done is done. I can't change the past, but—'

'But what? What exactly is your future at this point? And don't you *dare* say it's to learn that damned dress's make.' Dai Ma brushed away Zarene's attempted retort. 'You ought to be married by now. There are rumours, Zarene. They're spreading through all of Navaarat. Terrible rumours that soil your character and Maimoon Sahb's name. You may not be the wicked girl they claim you to be, but you must see the foolishness of your ways, how you're choosing to waste your time. If you don't settle on a suitor and marry soon, there's nothing you'll be able to do to keep people from thinking those rumours true.'

'Ma,' Zarene sighed, exasperated. She set the quill down and balled her fists to brace herself. 'I don't know how to explain it, but I can't set my mind on marriage again. Not now. I had so much time to prepare for Naksh, to imagine the life we'd have and what our children would look like … I just can't go through all that with another man. I'll bear it, the burden of this … this failure, but I won't let a few stupid rumours and hearsay command my actions.'

'Oh, but you *are* willing to let a dress wrought from black magic tell you what to do?'

'I'm only listening to my instincts.' If an appetite for vindication and a panel of embroidery counted as instinct.

Eyes brimming with tears, Dai Ma scoffed. 'You haven't seen enough to know what instinct is.' She made to storm out, but halted at the hall's threshold. 'Your failure is not yours alone. It is mine as well.'

A sharp pang of guilt speared through Zarene. She grappled for words, all of which seemed to get lodged in her throat. 'I truly am sorry,' she managed, 'but this is what I am, and I don't know what else there is I *can* do.'

Dai Ma pinched her lips together harshly and left. Zarene took a moment to suppress the tumult of anger, sadness and loneliness flaring up inside her. She opened the household accounts ledger, but could hardly read any of the figures because of her bleary vision. Pawing her eyes, sniffling, she willed the tears away, only to have her heart plummet to new depths.

There was a grand amount her father had set aside in his budget. It was to host a celebration at Mani Kot in honour of his newly-married daughter and his son by law.

❋

Without the aid of Dai Ma's experienced hand, Zarene was tested to her limits. Not only did she have to decide on the mela's every minute detail, but she also had to personally oversee if things were going to plan. Reminding herself she was her father's daughter, she wore a brave face while striking reasonable deals with construction labourers, cooks, sweet-makers, animal wranglers and suppliers of every known stripe.

She was on the move from dawn till well past sundown, and after dinner, the household servants would hound her with grievances about outsiders intruding upon their domain. Zarene spent the rest of her evenings cross-checking expenses to ensure she did not run over budget. When she retired late at night, she hardly slept. It was all too much, and everything seemed poised to come crashing down on her. Still, she had to go on. She needed answers.

Rahi, Dai Ma's youngest daughter, was the first of the girls to arrive with her infant son. Zarene bounded out of the haveli and practically leapt on her in greeting. She pressed Rahi flush against her in a hug and breathed a sigh of relief. The bleakness weighing on her began to dissipate, and the mammoth task she had undertaken seemed less daunting.

Things got better still when Kalindi and Pakhi arrived. Having grown up in Mani Kot alongside Zarene, they soon slipped into their old ways. The items on Zarene's daily agenda were redistributed into four equal parts. But while the work *was* a priority (it was completed with the greatest care and precision), nothing was more important than their mealtimes together.

They spent hours laughing—at old memories, lewd jokes, stories of awkward encounters, antics of the girls' husbands and children, and the many complex intrigues and forbidden romances vexing the residents of Mani Kot. Some days, their meals were so long drawn out, it was a wonder they got any work done at all. But Zarene didn't worry. When she did eventually return her attention to preparations for the mela, nursing aching ribs, she carried on under the firm belief that all would be well.

The arrangements came together beautifully. At dawn on the first day of festivities, some of the purchased cattle were sacrificed for the dinner courses. After performing the sacrificial rites, Mani Kot's cleric blessed the grounds with prayer and spritzes of rose water. Vast as the Mani Kot estate was, this took longer than expected. By the time the gates were finally opened, Zarene worried everyone in the growing crowd gathered outside might curse her.

Children and their parents flooded into the grounds like a monsoon surge. Every one of them halted in their tracks, traded looks of disbelief, and squealed in delight. Zarene swelled with pride as she saw the same realization dawn on all their faces: this was more than just a free meal. It was something most of them could never dream of—a week of pure, unabashed enjoyment.

A small city of awnings covered the estate's expansive lawns. Sherbet makers wove through the maze of stalls and attractions, distributing drinks from trays slung from their shoulders. The guests sipped on lemonade and coconut water timidly, jarred by the generosity on display, unsure where to even begin.

Because Zarene needed time to sift through the children, she and her sisters had come up with various incentives to keep them on the grounds. They set up stalls holding gifts by the gates. Each child was to receive one present for every day they attended. On the first day, the stalls held colourful glass bangles for the girls, and leather satchels for the boys.

Further in, there were games—ball and ring tosses, sack and egg races, fishing drums—and monkey wranglers, snake charmers and fire performers. Past them lay the crafts stalls—Zarene had assigned accomplished miniaturists, figurine-and kite-makers, and embroiderers to man them. Then came the contortionist's tent, and beside it a small window stage for puppet shows. The singers and drummers, though free to move about, chose to station themselves here as well. They taught the children to sing along with their choruses, and rounded them up with a boisterous musical number before the puppet shows began.

The mouthwatering aroma of Navaarati delicacies wafted out from the heart of the coiling maze of awnings. Among the outer loops of food stalls were the sweetmeats and snacks. Fresh jilapi batter was piped into hot oil, the crispy pastry then dunked in sugar syrup. Fat, pillow-soft gulaab jamuns bobbled in cauldrons of saffron-infused sugar syrup. Eight varieties of halwa and five types of shandesh were garnished with cashews and pistachios, then cut into precise, diamond-shaped portions. Countless types of pithas—deep-fried, wheel-shaped dumplings stuffed with coconut, rice wraps stuffed with saturated milk pudding—were put on display in round dalas.

At the very heart of the grounds, midday meals and dinners were served in batches of fifty under the two largest awnings. Seating guests in orderly rows, servers spooned generous helpings of food onto large banana leaves. Freshly caught carp prepared with mustard and coconut milk, deep-fried tilapia, thick and creamy daal, tomato shrimp, mashed green beans and shrimp, and an entire litany of vegetable and paneer preparations were served in the afternoons. In the evenings, there was biryani—mutton, and vegetable. Sheekh kebabs, spiced chicken quarters, vegetable, corn and paneer sheekhs. Korma and rezala. Raita, borhani and lassi to cut through the grease.

Zarene had arranged for partitions to separate seating for the nobility and well-to-do from that of the common folk, but it was for nought. Following the wedding debacle and the scene at the mehfil, none of Zarene's peers—people who once clamoured for her attention—had accepted her invitation. Not even out of curiosity. Zarene was stung by the nastiness of it. There were times thinking of it made her feel like her clothes had suddenly shrunk and she could not breathe. But to dwell on it, to allow it to make her melancholy was too exhausting. What good was it, worrying about what others thought of her? She could only be master of her own judgements. Tilting her chin up, she made her rounds about the grounds.

❋

The festive air at Mani Kot was contagious. Zarene soon forgot about her troubles and began enjoying all that the mela had to offer. She joined the children while watching the puppet shows, helped them with their embroidery, and even distributed jilapis and other snacks. Parents approached her often to tell her of their woes. Sometimes she was able to make promises of help; other times she could do little but nod in sympathy. Either way, they always thanked her and took her leave with a promise to remember her in their prayers.

On the mela's third day, Zarene made her way to the outermost awnings on a routine walkabout. She was stopped every few steps by parents bearing gifts of fruit and flowers, hands working stalls, and excited children intent on showing her their handiwork. A throng of children encircled her to sing her a song they'd just learnt. Fragments of a nearby argument cut through their energetic, if a little shrill, notes.

'... no swindling under the bibi's good graces, you hear? Off you go, before I clip your ear. Go on!'

'Come now, Kaka. What's another set of clothes to a rich woman, yeah?' The retorting voice was soft. A child's. 'She can buy herself another hundred if she likes.'

Craning her neck to peer over the gathered children, Zarene spotted a boy, no older than twelve by his looks, at the gift stall for girls. He had on a white turban and wore an olive knee-length robe three times his size. The woven, mossy brown patterns along the robe's collar and opening down the front were distinctly northern—that of a chhuba coat, if she was not mistaken. Its material looked too light for the harsh northern winter, though, and the garment was missing its signature sash around the waist.

The stout, moustached man working the stall sat on a low stool before his wares. He shoved a set of clothes into an entering girl's hands and did so quickly so the boy could not snatch anything. 'She can, yes. But I'll not risk my neck by breaking orders for the likes of you.'

'What's that supposed to mean?'

'Destroyer's serpents take you, boy,' the man huffed. He pointed at the neighbouring stall. 'Just take a pair of sandals and leave me be.'

'I'd already told you, though, I've got a little brother and two sisters.'

'Well, then you should'a brought 'em with you.'

'Zarene!'

The children around her quieted. A few determined souls raised their voices and continued singing, bearing all their technical shortcomings. Zarene whipped her head back and did a double take. A small, finely clad woman, clutching her orna with one hand and a child with the other, threaded her way through the cluster of children. Her wide lips pulled up in a toothy, gleeful smile that took up half her face.

'Romila,' Zarene said, momentarily speechless. 'What are you doing here?'

Romila was one of the few girls Zarene could call a friend growing up. Though they were the same age, Romila had married several years earlier, to a man nearly twice her age and very plain of face. She was courteous when it was announced Zarene would marry Naksh, but her conspicuous withdrawal from Zarene's company told a different story. Zarene imagined she must have relished Naksh riding into the palace with Tumpa instead of her.

Romila rose to the tips of her toes and hugged her awkwardly. 'I would've come sooner, believe me. But, oh, I don't know! There's been such a row on what to do with you, and well … it's all quite silly when you think about it, so I just decided to grow a spine and come. Destroyer take what everyone says! Who cares?' She pulled on her son's arm. 'And Isham is so excited. Aren't you, my love?'

Zarene looked down at the boy—a spitting image of his father. Disguising her grimace with a smile, she said, 'This can't be Isham. You've grown so big!'

The boy gaped at her, clutching a pair of gift sandals to his chest. Something in his vacant eyes made Zarene glance back at the gift stall. The moustached man had risen from his stool to stretch his legs. The boy in the turban and chhuba was gone.

'Well, I won't keep you from all the fun.' Struggling to tear her eyes from the stall, she said to Romila, 'I would accompany you, but I need to see if everything is running in order. Maybe I'll join you for dinner.'

'Yes, let's do that,' Romila said, a little too animated.

Zarene shot her a trite smile and quickly slipped past her and the congregated children.

The moustached man stiffened and bowed on seeing her approach.

'All well, Chacha?'

'Yes, Bibi,' he replied, his eyes cast down and palms pressed together in a show of respect.

'That boy who was just here—'

'A trouble-maker, Bibi, but I took care of it.'

'Where did he go?'

'In, I reckon. Forgive me, Bibi, I wasn't looking. I'll go find him for you.'

'That's all right. You stay where you are. I'll get one of the guards to seek him out.'

'I made sure he didn't steal anything.'

'There's nothing to steal here, Chacha. This is all meant for them. Don't worry, it's nothing. Truly.'

Flashing him a reassuring smile, Zarene flagged down the nearest guard and asked him to search the grounds for the boy.

As promised, Zarene joined Romila for dinner and brought her foster sisters as reinforcements. Romila bristled at having to share a meal with the low-born daughters of a nursemaid, while Zarene tolerated little Isham's penchant for spraying food from his mouth with thinly veiled disdain. With the starter course of luchi and aloo dum cleared, bearers were in the process of serving biryani when a guard apologetically cleared his throat to get Zarene's attention.

Heart aflutter, Zarene inhaled sharply. 'Did you find him?'

The man's brows knotted. 'I don't understand, Bibi.'

Zarene shook her head. 'Never mind, what is it?'

'There um … there's been a rider, Bibi. From Jonglan Kot.'

'That's Shurram's estate, isn't it?' Pakhi inquired.

Zarene groaned. What did that horrid man want now? The glimmer of interest in Romila's eyes did not escape her. 'And? What does he come bearing?'

'News, Bibi … of Laal Shurram Sahb's death.'

Silence. Eyes widened and jaws turned slack. Disbelief muffled the noise of merriment beyond the dining area's partition.

'To Creator we shall all return,' Rahi was the first to say.

The others followed suit.

'But he and my husband were together only last night,' Romila said. 'Al-kran didn't mention he was ill.'

'He was killed, Bibi … erm, Sahiba,' the guard said. 'His hunting party was ambushed by bandits.'

'Bandits? In Shandrabad?' Romila pulled Isham flush against her side.

Zarene refrained from rolling her eyes. Her father had always said murderers and thieves would remain a constant so long as the divide between rich and poor, and between Pajcathis and Khalaqans prevailed. Shandrabad, for all its outward serenity, was no different from the rest of Navaarat. The only reason her wedding procession had not been ambushed in the jungle was because royal soldiers had been posted along the route to the river.

'Have they captured the culprits?' asked Zarene.

'No, Bibi. Those who survived fled to safety, and the snakes were long gone by the time they returned with more men.'

'Creator save us all,' Romila chanted under her breath, squeezing her son's head to her bosom. 'Murderers roaming free in Shandrabad. How is any mother to sleep at night? And the mela!' She gasped theatrically, 'Zarene, you'll have to shut it down.'

There were a number of responses Zarene wished to spit at Romila. That Shurram was likely killed by one of his own tenants. That she had taken every precaution to ensure the safety of the attending families. That none of this was her business. But all of it went unsaid as she felt a hand squeeze her balled fist.

'She's right,' Pakhi said, softly. 'Shurram was an esteemed courtier in the raja's service. The whole of Shandrabad will be expected to go into mourning for the coming month. For the mela at Mani Kot to continue would be a show of grave disrespect.'

Zarene pinched her lips together to stave off the tears burning her eyes, to keep herself from bellowing 'no!' and accusing them all of purposely sabotaging her mela, of wanting to see her fail. But the look of pity on Pakhi, Rahi and Kalindi's faces confirmed there was no way around it. Aware of Romila's keen gaze trained on her, Zarene bit into her bottom lip and pulled on a mask of indifference. She cleared her throat to rid it of tremors, and addressed the guard.

'No, of course the mela can't continue. Besides, Shurram was a man of such high regard that I doubt anyone will be in any mood to make merry. Spread word that tonight is to be the mela's last. The workers will be paid all seven days' wages.'

Pakhi rubbed her thumb up and down Zarene's hand, but it was no comfort. Bearers resumed their serving duties. Eyes stinging, Zarene couldn't tell what was being ladled onto her banana leaf. The aroma of the food turned her stomach, and something pushed its way up her throat. When the choking sensation became unbearable, she rose to her feet and excused herself.

The estate grounds blurred as she broke into a run, dodging and swerving past chirping children, hollering workers, and clattering pots, pans and trays. Trails of light tapered out to darkness, and busy sounds gave way to the steady chirps of crickets. She didn't know if she was alone. She didn't care. Falling to her knees, hugging her stomach, she uttered a hoarse wail. The dam crumbled and angry tears spilt forth. Her fingers dug into the soft earth under the grass as the rest of her convulsed until she was gasping for air.

Her heart felt too large for her chest. At the same time, it felt like it was being sucked of all its substance. She rolled onto her back and begged for the shivers to stop. Through shuddering breaths, she wished for a simpler life; one where every one of her plans was not thwarted beyond repair. Overhead, a part of the sky sparkled with starlight. The braziers and cook fires from the mela blotted the rest of it pitch black.

Truth was, she had a simple life once. She had just made the mistake of complicating it by wanting the unattainable.

When the worst of her attack subsided, Zarene sat up and took her bearings. She had run all the way to her rose garden. Some small part of her must have still hoped she'd find what she was looking for before it was too late. She would have chuckled at the absurdity of it if her head wasn't throbbing. A soft, pained yelp escaped her lips as she picked herself up.

She kept telling herself it could be worse. How many people had the luxury of a private rose garden to cry in? In full bloom, the flowers had a subtly sweet scent that helped settle Zarene's stomach. Still hugging herself, Zarene strolled along the neat grid of gravel paths between rose bushes. The voices of servants and attendees from the grounds melded together, almost sounding like approaching rainclouds. Things could indeed be worse. She was very fortunate.

The path opened out to a small square lawn. Rising from its right was a section of the family quarters. A flight of steep marble stairs led up to a balcony enclosed by white balustrades. Faint candlelight, from Zarene's bedchamber beyond it, fell on the lawn, casting lopsided shadow-beams over the grass and bushes.

Hiking up the hem of her saree, Zarene was about to climb up the stairs when something flashed on the far side of the lawn. She followed the strip of light and squatted to extricate a slender object hastily shoved under a rosebush.

It was a silver smoking pipe that ran a little longer than Zarene's legs. A few simple floral motifs were engraved on its surface. The gardener must have stolen—well, borrowed it—from her father's study. It wasn't all that surprising for his absence and her own preoccupation with the mela to embolden some of the servants. It wasn't a big deal. Tomorrow, everything would go back to as it was.

Sighing, Zarene blew into the pipe. The air did not pass. She clicked her tongue and stuck a finger into the spout on the other end. It seemed fine. But then, she was hardly an authority on smoking pipes. Using it as a walking stick, she headed inside.

❈

Stupid Shurram! What a nuisance, even in death!

The sentiment nagged at Zarene like a splinter as she tossed and turned in bed. The man had laid waste to her hard work, and he didn't even have the decency to stay alive so she could wish him ill.

Stupid, odorous man!

Her curses carried over to her fitful dreams, where they chased her through stampeding elephants and dry stepwells and lush underground groves. When she came face to face with the plum giantess, instead of her own reflection, she saw Shurram's black mouth sneering back at her.

I'll remember to keep you in my prayers, Sahiba.

A feather brushed against Zarene's hand. She flicked it away. The sheets shifted underneath her. Half asleep, she shuffled her feet to anchor herself and groaned irritably. The motion stilled a moment before she was tossed sideways, onto the mosquito net encasing her bed. The thin material gave way under her weight, tearing and—

'Ow!' she cried as she crashed into the hard marble floor.

Pain pulsed through her left arm and hip. Propping herself up on her elbow, she blinked away any remnants of sleep. Hovering over the bed, tented and fluttering as though a breeze cut through the chamber, was the muslin orna. Her eyes flew to the armoire where she had stowed it with the ghagra. Its door was closed. Gritting her teeth, she tried to snatch it from the air. It folded, swerved and twisted, evading her every attempt.

There is a song they will not hear. Her blood sang. *Savour it and trust it you must.*

Zarene growled in irritation. Brandishing the orna aside, she raised a leg to climb back into bed. The orna spread out to its full expanse, swathed her whole, and latched onto her.

'No, let go!' Zarene gasped, limbs resisting the tightening fabric around her. The orna pushed her farther and farther away from the bed. Her bare heels squeaked against the marble. A faint light intruded on the cozy darkness of her chamber. Starlight, Zarene realized, a mere moment before the orna pinned her against the balcony's balustrades. She pushed back and did her best to keep her feet planted as it bent her torso over the edge.

The fabric muffled her screams, bore down on her throat till she almost choked.

Then, just like that, the life drained from it. It slid down her trembling body and collected in a white pool at her feet. Fingers clasping at her tender throat, coughing, she kicked it away and stared at it. It just lay there like a benign article of clothing.

Zarene peered over the balustrade. Would the fall have killed her? Most likely not. A morbid chuckle passed her lips as she thought of what people would have thought if she *had* been thrown off. A failed suicide for a failed mela. Or worse, for a failed betrothal and a dead suitor.

Her chest slumped. For the second time that night, she called on the scent of the roses from the garden below to calm her nerves. She basked in the stillness of the view before her, a sharp contrast to her nagging thoughts and tumultuous dreams. Her eyes grew bleary with sleep and her yawns became more insistent. Pushing herself off the balustrade, she took one last whiff of the sweet scent.

Something rustled. A shadow shaped like an oversized frog dawdled along the edges of the lawn. Zarene's head whipped down to the balcony's floor, where the orna still lay—lifeless. Squinting back at the lawn, she realized the figure was loitering about the same spot where she had found her father's pipe.

The gardener.

Shaking her head, she made her way down the stairs and crept up behind the figure. 'Is something the matter, Chacha?'

The figure sprang to his feet, hands out in a defensive stance. Not the gardener. Not even a man grown. It was a child in a turban, with an abnormally large and pudgy torso. One hand still up to ward off an attack, he clasped his chest protectively, shifting his weight from heel to toe.

'Who are you?' Zarene edged closer. 'What are you doing here at this hour?'

The boy straightened and cleared his throat to answer. 'Erm ...'

He bounded off into the rose bushes.

'Hey! Come back here! Guards!'

Zarene gave chase, unperturbed by the gashes thorns cut into her kaftan and skin. The inside of her thighs chafed from friction. Her lungs were ablaze. But while the child was lithe and swift, he was unfamiliar with the lay of Mani Kot, which kept Zarene from losing him. 'Intruder! Intruder in the grounds! Guards!'

The grounds stirred. Her shouts received a few groggy answers, but the route of her pursuit remained empty. The child led her to the lawns, where many of the awnings had already been taken down. Slithering through the disarray, he leapt from a stall table and grabbed an awning's bamboo frame. After a few swings back and forth, he wheeled his feet up and onto the awning's canvas roof. He bounced to test the surface, then looked about frantically.

'Hey, you! Get down from there! Guards! Guards! Over here!'

Wringing his wrists as if they were wet, he took a few steps back. Breaking into a brisk run, he hollered as he leapt off the framed edge of the canvas. He landed on a solid surface—a rooftop. The guest house's rooftop.

Zarene took a few steps back, rose to the tip of her toes and craned her neck. He was heading for a dark, swaying cloud on the other side of the building. Her breath lodged in her throat as she realized what he was about to do. Turning on her heel, she bolted, not to the building's other side, but far past it to Mani Kot's bamboo enclosure. Unlatching a small servant's gate, she trudged through unkempt grass and mud and followed the fence until she was under the black cloud—a mango tree, the largest there was in Mani Kot.

Pressing herself flush against the fence, concealing herself in the tree's shade, Zarene set her sights on the burly branches that spilt over the enclosure. Soon enough, a rustle sounded in the thick mass of leaves and a bulge of white atop billowing robes squeezed out from it. Zarene moved into position.

The figure fluttered to the ground with a soft *thump*. She pounced and pinned him to the ground with all her weight.

'Let go of me!' The child bucked against her.

'Why were you in my garden? I mean you no h-harm. Just … just … ugh, just hold still, boy.'

'Zarene Bibi! Where are you?' the guards called from within. 'Zarene Bibi!'

'Over here!' She groaned as the child elbowed her in the stomach. 'Outside! Hurry!'

FIVE

It took the combined strength of two guards to drag the boy to the pillared study hall. Another guard collected the articles that had fallen out of his olive chhuba and laid them out on the long table. Zarene sat down at the end of one of the benches and ordered the guards to unhand the boy.

'But, Bibi…'

'It's all right.' To the boy, she said, 'I mean you no harm, understand? I just have a few questions. Then you can take your things and be on your way. Good?'

One of the guards jerked him. Stifling a whimper, he nodded.

'Release him.'

The guards shoved him forward, but they made no move to back away. The boy's breath hitched with fear. Pouting, he intertwined his fingers and nervously jabbed one thumb at the other. Saffron pantaloons peeked out from underneath his chhuba. His shins were strapped in leather greaves.

Under patches of brown suntan, he was fair of skin. The plains of his face—his cheeks, chin and forehead—were flat. Its immaculately straight ridges looked sculpted with the aid of a measuring rod. He had a small rectangular chin, wide dusty pink lips that parted like a coffer's lid, and short lashes bleached by sunlight.

Zarene drummed her fingers against the table. She mussed her lips together, trying to think of something that would put the child at ease. 'I … uh … I climbed that tree once myself … did it to sneak off the grounds during lessons. Of course, I hadn't thought of a way back in, so I had to come back through the gates all muddied up. Earned myself a good thrashing that day.'

Sucking a deep breath, the boy said, 'I want to leave.'

Zarene's eyes darted to the door leading out and the corridor past it. She nodded. 'Soon. But first tell me why you were in my garden in the dead of night.'

'I wasn't taking nothing, yeah? I swear!' His speech was riddled with northern inflections. 'I only came because I'd left something there—my pipe. I hid it in a bush 'cause I didn't want nobody thinking I'd stole it.'

'The little rat's lying,' one of the guards growled.

Zarene raised a hand to silence him. 'That pipe looked an awful lot like one of my father's.'

'It does not!' The boy's eyes lit up with indignation. 'It's mine, and it was my Baa's before me.'

'You'll have to forgive me for not believing that.' After a pause, she added, 'But I'll check to see if what you say is true.'

The boy pursed his lips. His glare made Zarene check the door behind him once more. What was taking the girls so long?

She studied the pile of articles on the table before her: A sash whose pattern matched that of the boy's chhuba, a few copper daulatis, a tawdry ring, an apple, a pair of sandals much too small for him and three sets of girls' clothes from the gift stall.

'That's odd. Didn't you say you had one brother and only two sisters?'

Growing rigid, the boy tried to hold his glare, but his right eye twitched. Zarene took in the strands of stick-straight hair that escaped his turban, the oversized chhuba that concealed the shape of his body. Her mouth froze half open as she suppressed a gasp of surprise.

'Leave us,' she ordered the guards.

'Bibi?'

'Do as I say.'

'We'll be outside.' To the child, one of them said, 'Try anything and it'll be your neck.'

'So …' Once she made sure the guards were out of earshot, Zarene's lips pulled up in a conspiratorial smile. 'I know your secret.'

'Give me back my pipe!'

'Is it to complete your disguise? But who do you wish to fool? Who are you, little one?'

'I'm not little. I'm fourteen.'

'Almost a woman, then. I suppose dressing like a lad helps keep unwanted eyes off. Especially if one's wont to sneaking in and out of places.'

'Hey, you're the one opening your grounds to everyone and their fourteen fathers.'

Zarene chuckled at the strange adage. 'I didn't open the garden. You're not from here, are you? If you were, your brother and sisters would have come here themselves.'

'What's that got to do with anything?'

'I don't know,' Zarene sighed. She did not have much to go on. 'Just making conversation, I suppose. At least tell me your name. I'm Zarene.'

'Everyone and their mother knows that,' the girl chided. After an exasperated pause, she gave in. 'Keyan.'

'And your real name?'

'You're not my mother.'

'Fair enough.' Hurried steps sounded from the corridor outside. 'Ah,' Zarene breathed in relief. 'Here we are.'

In marched her foster sisters with Kalindi in the middle. The ghagra was slung like a hammock between her outstretched forearms. The orna hung messily from the crook of Pakhi's arm, part of its edge brushing the floor. There was a quick exchange of inquiring looks between them and Zarene.

Zarene pushed aside Keyan's paltry belongings and loot for Kalindi to splay the ghagra over the table. It drew a confounded hiccup from Keyan.

'Pretty, isn't it? Have you seen anything like it? A speciality where you hail from, perhaps?'

'Where I—?' Keyan laughed. Her open palm hovered just above the material. 'It flows like clear and cold water coming down from the mountains. That's all there is where I come from. I've never seen anything like this. And before you accuse me of wanting to steal it, I'll have you know I've got no use for it. Nobody I know does.'

Though her feet pivoted, Keyan's eyes stayed glued on the ghagra, mesmerized. A finger, its nail chewed and rimmed with dirt, guided her gaze from one panel to the next like she was reading. Zarene clasped and unclasped her hands together, waiting with bated breath.

Kalindi had set the ghagra down so the final panel was the first thing the eyes went to. It did not interest Keyan, though. Her gaze slid left to the events that preceded it: the botched wedding, the wedding procession itself, Tumpa receiving the egg from—

The rest spilt over the ghagra's edge, onto the side facing down. Fingers twitching to flip it over, Keyan pulled her hand away. 'It's a story, then? Of a bride tricked by a funny stranger?'

'Something like that. Is it a common tale where you're from?'

Keyan snorted. 'Women don't go 'bout stealing others' husbands where I'm from.' Her finger moved higher. 'Hey, there's more than one story here.'

It had never occurred to Zarene that there could be some order to the crowds of indistinguishable figures around the account of her own misfortune. But seeing Keyan's finger halt at a group of hunters, she was ashamed not to have thought of it sooner. Their bows were pointed in the direction from which Tumpa received her egg, their prey cut off by the ghagra's edge.

'Here,' Zarene flipped the ghagra to show her the other side. 'Just take a good, hard look and tell me if *any* of the stories, *anything* you see looks familiar.'

The tiniest tremor shot through Keyan. A low whimper escaped her lips. 'Who's that?'

She was pointing at the plum giantess. The thread used to craft her shimmered in the candlelight. She looked ethereal, though not quite as magnificent as she did in Zarene's dreams. One of the twelve smaller scions she ripped herself into was prey to the party of hunters. Zarene shuddered as she followed the hunters dragging her corpse in a manner unfit even for slaughtered livestock. They mounted it for display in a shrine.

'I was hoping you could tell me,' Zarene said, suddenly feeling her own sorrows quite trivial.

Face turning a splotchy red, Keyan tore her gaze from the ghagra and pulled away from the table. She was trembling all over and her hands were balled into fists. 'A witch is what she is. One that changes shape, makes herself look all nice to lure her prey, whispering all sorts of evil in his ear.'

'A master of disguise, hmm? So someone, say, like yourself?'

Keyan clicked her tongue in irritation. 'You people think all us mountain folk are shamans. But if I had a witch's power, do you think I'd keep asking you to give my pipe back? I'm telling you, I don't know none of these stories, and I'm telling you I want to leave! Keep the clothes, I don't want them. But I need my pipe.'

Zarene saw that beneath the wry and belligerent exterior, Keyan was terrified, almost to the brink of tears.

'There's something you're not telling me. Do you know how I know that?' Zarene turned the ghagra over again and showed her the wedding procession. 'Because this is my wedding. This is me, and this was the woman my betrothed made off with. And this,' she flattened the final panel, 'is you in my rose garden. I was *meant* to find you, Keyan.'

Scoffing, Keyan studied the panel. 'That looks nothing like me.'

She was not wrong. The child on the ghagra had shoulder-length hair and wore an ordinary beige tunic.

'You were the only child to show up in my garden.'

'Didi, I mean no disrespect, but a few pitchures on a garghi can't tell you what to do. And look, there's nothing after this, see? Someone's been making a right fool of you. If I were you, I'd destroy it and get on with my life. Now, just give me my pipe back so I can go, yeah?'

Zarene drew a long breath. She knew if the likes of Naksh or Dai Ma couldn't appreciate her fascination with the ensemble, Keyan wouldn't either. How could she, when she likely didn't know where her next meal would come from? Zarene needed to make a more convincing case for herself.

'That's the thing, Keyan, I can't destroy it. I've tried. See, the woman my betrothed made off with here? She's the princess of Shandrabad now, but she can't see to her duties. This dress whispered all sorts of evil in her ear, and it drove her mad. If you don't help me destroy it, she'll be that way forever. The city will fall into chaos.'

'Mad?' Keyan's harsh features softened, shedding years off her.

'It's terrible, really. I'd hate to think how everyone in Shandrabad will suffer because of this.' Zarene smiled sadly. 'But the ghagra will show us the way to make it right, I'm sure of it. Another panel will appear. My handmaids and Dai Ma can tell you this last panel wasn't here a month ago. We just need to give it some time, that's all. You'll have nothing to want for under my care.'

'But …' Keyan looked about the room, torn. 'I don't have a month, though. Please, I need my pipe back.'

'I'll send word to your family, wherever they are. They may come and stay at Mani Kot too.'

Jerking her head back in disbelief, Keyan considered the offer a moment, then shook her head. 'It'll take too long, and they'll not bring Baa with them,' she said, her voice thinly laced with regret. 'I have to go.'

The early morning call to prayer sounded outside. Flashes of Zarene's dreams returned to her: the cloud of dust leading to a stair-lined chasm, the weightlessness she felt as she fell, then flew.

'Then I'll come with you.'

'What?' Keyan baulked.

'Zarene!' Kalindi, Rahi and Pakhi gasped in unison.

'If I can't find my answers in Shandrabad, I'll have to find them elsewhere, just as I had to look beyond Mani Kot for the child.' She gave Keyan a once over. 'You said you're from the mountains. From your appearance, I'd wager you were from Barwasi or thereabouts.'

'Zarene,' Rahi hissed. 'You can't possibly go to Barwasi. Maimoon Sahb will never allow it.'

'Abba is not due back for another two months. He can't forbid me from doing something if I do it before he hears of it.'

'Zarene, this is madness.' Kalindi shot Keyan a withering glare. 'And don't you dare encourage her. You'll stay right here until we've found some use for you.'

'I-I'm not even going back to Barwasi,' Keyan stammered. 'N-not at first, at least. I've got to collect my reward.'

'Reward?' Zarene raised a brow. 'Reward for what?'

'Honest work, that's what. And none of your business.'

'Well? Where must you collect it from?'

'Reshumnagar.'

Face lighting up with a smug grin, Zarene twisted to look at her foster sisters. 'Home of the best silk market in Navaarat. Not to mention much closer than Barwasi.'

'I don't know, Zarene,' said Pakhi.

Savour it and trust it you must.

'No, this is right. I feel it. It's decided, then. I'll go to Reshumnagar.' Seeing Keyan open her mouth in protest, Zarene added, 'And just so you don't run off, I'll match your reward at Reshumnagar. How does that sound? Half now, half once I get my answers. How much are you being paid?'

Keyan crossed her arms. 'Twenty gold daulatis.'

'By Creator, girl, you didn't kill anyone! Come, don't take me for a fool. It doesn't cost more than seven silver copper daulatis for a courier to deliver something valuable from Reshumnagar to Shandrabad on short notice. You're not saying you delivered thirty-five parcels on your own, are you?'

'Hey, you're in no place to bargain, yeah? You want my help or not?'

Kalindi, Pakhi and Rahi shook their heads at Zarene as she calculated whether she could spare the expense.

'All right, then,' she said with a satisfied nod. 'Twenty gold daulatis. But you only get ten until I deem my work finished.'

❋

The pipe didn't belong to Zarene's father after all. She hesitated to return it to Keyan for fear she would run off, but she worried for nought. The pull of the ten gold daulatis kept Keyan rooted at Mani Kot as Zarene prepared for the journey west to Reshumnagar.

A rider was sent ahead to arrange for accommodations in Reshumnagar and along the way. Zarene decided to take a plain palanquin that wouldn't attract too much attention, and a retinue of three armed guards and four bearers in plainclothes. To the consternation of her sisters, she decided not to take any handmaids, and packed the ghagra and orna ensemble alongside the barest of essentials into a bundle secured by leather straps. The girls took great pains to weave and sew inconspicuous jute pockets into the palanquin's walls to stow coins in. Zarene also designed herself a purse to wear around her neck, under her clothes.

For her wardrobe, Zarene had her tailors make her loose, pleated salwars that tapered down at her ankles, and plain flowy kameezes of pure cotton that touched her knees. Each set came with matching *ornas*. She learnt to do her hair up in a turban with them so it didn't get dirty and require frequent washing. From her father's belongings, she retrieved an old mustard qaba coat, which was lined with cotton and embellished with light but intricate black detailing along the opening at the chest and at the cuffs. She used to make a tent out of it as a child. Now, its sleeves draped over her shoulders quite nicely and concealed her figure.

A week and a half after the mela's abrupt end, the inhabitants of Mani Kot gathered at one of the estate's side entrances to bid Zarene and her retinue farewell. Dai Ma was among them, her pretty eyes rimmed dark purple and glistening a blustery black.

Kalindi, Rahi and Pakhi veiled their worries with jests.

'Try not to get yourself killed,' Pakhi said.

'Don't spend everything you have on fabric,' Kalindi suggested. 'You have to bring back gifts for us.'

'Be wary of strange men. Don't go running off with them, no matter how charming they are,' Rahi giggled. Kalindi smacked her on the shoulder.

Turning to Dai Ma, Zarene smiled. She had held the tiniest sliver of hope that their standoff would draw to an end now that she was leaving, but when she wrapped her arms around her, it was as good as hugging a slab of stone.

'I'll take care of myself,' Zarene promised. 'Reshumnagar isn't that far anyway. When Abba returns, tell him I've taken every possible precaution and that he has no need to worry.'

Dai Ma extricated herself from her embrace. 'I'll have no part in this foolishness, Sahiba. I am only a lowly nursemaid you've chosen to punish in her old age.'

'Ma, please …'

'No,' she said, her voice hoarse. Her tired eyes bore down on her. 'No. It's your life. Yours to ruin. Go. Just go.'

'Ma—'

Turning on her heel, Dai Ma marched inside. Zarene brushed off her sisters' consolations and climbed into the palanquin. She rubbed her face raw as she wiped the hot tears spilling down from her eyes.

Alone in her palanquin with nothing but her thoughts and the steady *humma humma hums* of the bearers outside for company, Zarene's despair gave way to steely determination.

Steadfast and certain as solitude and dust.

SIX

Keyan dribbled a rock as she walked, alternating between the inside edges of her feet and the spout of her pipe. The game kept her from speeding ahead. Beside her, Zarene watched in envy.

The days were long and hot. Zarene opted to walk for the most part to relieve her bearers. She had tried mimicking Keyan once, but only succeeded in filling the soles of her sandals with pebbles.

Why didn't she have a pair of boots like Abba's made? The heat. That's what it was. Better to have a sandy foot than a stinky boot.

'Mind if I ask you something, Didi?'

'Hmm?' Zarene blinked as if she had been pulled from a daze. Keyan rarely spoke unless spoken to. Her irritation with the snail's pace of their journey usually manifested in hostile silence. 'Yes, of course. Ask away.'

'The girl who stole your groom … she's Shanderbad's princess now instead of you, but you still want to help her?'

Zarene followed the *swish, swish, crunch* of Keyan's foot kicking the rock. It was a small lie. One that would not harm the girl in any way. 'Yes.'

'Why, though?'

'Because … well, Naksh—the prince, I mean—he said some terrible things about me that day, and doing nothing is as good as proving him right.'

Not the whole truth, but not a complete lie either. Anger unfurled its wings in her chest as flashes of Naksh—of his feigned fondness of her during their betrothal, his brash decision to ruin her life, his pathetic outburst at the mehfil—flitted through her memory. She *did* want to prove him wrong. Her passions weren't a slight against her character, and there wasn't a day she didn't wish she could scream so in his face.

'Huh.' Keyan's head jerked back in contemplation. 'You mustn't have liked him so much.'

'Yes, so little that I'm *only* trying to save his precious peasant princess.'

'That's not what I mean. I'm just saying if I ever get a clear shot at revenge, I'd take it.'

Studying Keyan, Zarene wondered if she could understand what she wanted after all. Still, it seemed too late to come clean. 'Is there someone you wish to exact revenge on, little one?'

Keyan bristled. The pale patches on her face turned red, and her right eye twitched. 'You don't have to be the one getting punched to feel its pain. Wrong's got plenty of ways of finding you.'

Turning the pipe's stem in her palm, she shuffled the rock forward with its spout. The flicks of her wrists lacked their usual finesse.

Words eluded Zarene. Only the direst of circumstances could have forced a child of fourteen, a girl at that, to work so far from home, alone. The pay may have been good, but couriers made easy targets for bandits. Zarene wanted to help. She had tried prying details out of Keyan—about her siblings, her ailing father, her mountainous abode, her world—but every inquiry was deflected with vagueness, if not silence.

'A bard's song sung may ring empty,' Zarene muttered under her breath, kicking a spray of dirt into the air.

'What?'

'No, nothing. That pipe of yours ... did you get someone to have a look at it at Mani Kot?'

'I reckon they'd looked their fill when they checked if I'd stole it.'

'Oh no, it's yours, I'm certain. It's just that ... it didn't pass air when I checked.'

'I don't use it to smoke.'

'I've noticed. Still, you might want someone to take a look at it.' Smiling, she added, 'In case the urge strikes.'

Keyan shook her head, annoyed. 'It's fine as is.'

Zarene drifted awake with a sigh and a parched throat. She almost called Dai Ma to bring her a goblet of milk before remembering she was not at Mani Kot. They were spending the night at the haveli of an acquaintance of her father's. Her head still light from dreaming, it took her a moment to recall where exactly the haveli was. Uttering a long, annoyed groan helped sharpen her senses. The bed creaked as she sat up; it was hard and made her ache all over.

Her heart hammered as it always did when she woke mid-dream. She retained no recollection of it, but knew what it was about: a stampede of elephants, a cavernous stepwell, a dark grove, and *her*—the plum giantess with no face who still managed to be so beautiful. Her words coursed through Zarene, spilt from her lips like a chant.

There is a song they will not hear.

A strain so strange and yet so dear.

She felt about the bed linens to see if the orna had slithered its way to her again. Finding nothing, she slipped onto the floor and unstrapped her bundle to rummage for the ghagra. To see if another panel had appeared.

There was nothing.

They were only three days away from Reshumnagar. Three days away from acquiring the fabrics needed to replicate the ensemble. A part of her relished the tangible prospect of humiliating Naksh, but another part of her found it odd that the garb's sole purpose was to direct her to the correct market. It felt like things were ending before they even started. She wanted more, but could not say what of.

Folding the ghagra along its pleats, she rolled it up and arranged it into a neat stack with the rest of her belongings. A series of distant huffing grunts and the rhythmic slices of metal against stone interrupted her efforts to rewrap her bundle. Following the sound to the gallery outside her chambers, she looked over the balustrade into the courtyard below.

By the dim light of a single lamp, Keyan danced to the rhythm of her own chants and the gentle taps, slices and swishes of her pipe. Her straight wet hair fell to her shoulders, darkening her loose white tunic with a damp patch. She was quick on her feet, and even quicker maneouvering the pipe in the air. The fluidity of her routine rendered her a blur, every definitive move—a jab forward, a cut sideways, a two-handed block—punctuated with a flitting *yah* or a resounding *huah*. Most mesmerizing was the way in which she spun the pipe, first on one side, then switching hands without compromising the motion.

Zarene watched, transfixed. She had heard that mountain folk employed methods of meditation different from those in Navaarat, but this was more than that. This was self-defence—the reason Keyan had survived working as a courier. Zarene marvelled at the sheer focus, discipline and time her training must have required. Soon, the rhythm of Keyan's manoeuvres synchronized with the words thrumming through her.

Savour it and trust it you must.

Steadfast and certain as solitude and dust.

The words ceased all of a sudden. As did Keyan. Gripped by a tightness in her chest, Zarene shrank into the gallery's shadows just as Keyan looked up. It felt wrong seeing her like that, as though she had intruded on something deeply private. Prayers were meant for no one but one's God, after all.

She scurried back to her chambers, wondering if she did so out of respect for Keyan or for the shame of her own prayers.

Reshumnagar was renowned for Surjalok Chowk, a market located at the city's heart. But Zarene and her retinue didn't have to go as far to taste the first bursts of glistening colour, and the sometimes fresh, sometimes acetic scent of new fabrics. The entire city teemed with vendors selling silks. They traded along narrow sandstone streets which were kept immaculately clean—no dirt or stray animals—so the merchandise stayed in pristine condition. Tea, coffee and sharbat sellers milled about, waiting to be flagged down by merchants looking to keep customers by their wares a while longer.

Zarene didn't need the lure of complimentary sharbat to keep looking, of course. If not for her exhausted escorts, and Keyan's scorching disdain burning a hole in her back, she would have gladly spent their first evening at Reshumnagar exploring what the city had to offer. The next morning, Zarene tucked the ghagra inside her qaba and gave her men the day off, hoping to browse Surjalok Chowk in peace.

To Zarene's dismay, Keyan caught her leaving and tagged along. A spring in her step, she appeared more excited than Zarene did herself.

'Just think of the sight it'll make,' Keyan said, taking strides so long Zarene had to jog to keep up. Better than a regular burning, that's for sure. Maybe they've got some special clippers or something, or oh! Maybe they'll call to the spirits in a nighttime ritual to break its curse!'

A dark cloud descended on Zarene's spirit. What if they did encounter someone who knew how to destroy the ghagra? Would she let them do it, or could she be brave enough to tell Keyan the truth? She didn't know.

By the time they approached the chowk's first shop, Zarene had forgotten how to speak. She dodged the merchant's friendly query about what she was looking for by pointing at random bolts of fabric. Shaking her head, she mumbled words like softer, stronger, finer, smoother. The merchant dutifully pulled out more bolts from his shelves. 'No harm in just looking,' he kept saying. But nothing matched the ghagra's material.

'That's all right, Chacha, don't take out any more,' she smiled, her heart pummelling against her ribs. 'I'll just have a look around.'

'Hey, no.' Keyan placed a hand on Zarene's arm. 'Show him the garghi.'

'No, really, I think we should just—'

'Uff!' Sticking her hand into Zarene's qaba, Keyan yanked out the ghagra and unfurled it over the display counter. 'Kaka, have you got anything like this?'

'Keyan!'

A whistle pierced through the merchant's throat. 'Well, I … by Mothers' fortune! If this isn't just so exquisite.'

Wiggling his fingers in the air, he scooped handfuls of the ghagra and passed them through his fingers. A moan of pleasure drawled from his lips. 'Oh! It's crisp but so soft. And, oh-ho-ho, it's not wrinkling! Why ... where ... how ... did you come by such a thing?'

'Never mind how. Do you know who'd made it? A weaver or a ... a ... what are they called? Sewers?'

'I don't think I ... although no, wait.' The merchant caressed the fabric, pressed it to his chest. 'I might have something like this in my storehouse. It'll take some time to retrieve, of course. I'll tell you what, why don't you just leave this with me for now and come back in a day or two?'

'You're certain it's this exact material with the layered effect?' Zarene asked, the pounding now in her ears.

'Now how can a man be certain of such a thing, Didi? I only know what my two eyes see.'

'Well, we're not here for more of the same cloth, are we?' Keyan snatched the ghagra from the merchant and returned it to Zarene. 'We'll be going now.'

Zarene looked forlornly over her shoulder as Keyan prodded her to the next shop with her pipe.

'Crooks. All of 'em,' she heard Keyan say. 'Would've served him right if we'd given it to him, though.'

Shops further down the line held more of the same wares. A few pieces caught Zarene's eye, but none of them served her purpose. The silk satins were not sheer enough; the chiffons and gauzes were too dainty to support embroidery; the organza wrinkled too easily; the crepes and georgettes were too grainy; and every piece with a woven pattern came in a single layer instead of the ghagra's many.

Despite Zarene's pleas to be discreet, Keyan brandished the ghagra at merchants, determined to find the people responsible for its creation. The garment elicited more of the same excitement and hunger. A few merchants—older men, and the rare women—stiffened at the sight of it, though, and could not shoo the girls away fast enough.

By the turn of an hour, Zarene was sure the entire market was tracking Keyan and her movements. The jitters, along with the fear of actually finding someone capable of destroying the ghagra, made her wonder if she shouldn't just buy a few bolts of fabric and declare the day a success.

Under the sun's midday glare, the baking sandstone heated Zarene's sandals and seared the soles of her feet. Inside the thick turban, her head felt like a steaming kettle without a spout that was ready to burst. Lugging her feet from one shop to the next, Zarene wrinkled and clinched her nose at the noxious body odour enveloping them. The people of Reshumnagar took pride in their silks. It did not matter to them that silks were not suitable for hot weather.

The combination of body odour and their midday meal of kathi rolls and mango lassi turned her stomach. Her throat burnt with the acrid taste of nausea. Hugging the ghagra and her purchases to her stomach, it took Zarene all her willpower not to keel over. A rough, steadying hand caught hold of her as her knees were about to buckle.

'The haveli's too far away,' Keyan said. She barked and brandished her free hand at bystanders to clear the way. 'Come to Polki Ghar with me, yeah?' she said to Zarene softly. 'It'll be nice and empty, and the air smells like the flowers in the gardens back in your Shanderbad. Don't lose heart, Didi. I'll make sure you find a way to take care of the garghi.'

The groan that Zarene uttered was not so much of pain as it was of guilt.

❈

Though a faint stench of burning skin and sweat still lingered in the air, Zarene guzzled the fresh air once they were clear of Surjalok Chowk. The heat still burnt her lungs, but anything was better than the fowl burn of a few moments ago. Her stomach was somewhat settled by the time they arrived at the gates of Polki Ghar, though her feet tripped over each other and her senses were adrift from her head staying captive inside her turban.

'I've got a reward to collect from Palmyr Sahb,' Keyan told the guard.

'And your friend here?'

'A tailor. See?' Keyan pinched the fabric in Zarene's arms.

'A little womanly for Sahbji, no?'

Keyan clicked her tongue. 'Ho Kaka,' she replied with her thick northern inflection, 'you know Sahbji's binnuch better than I do.'

'He makes no secret of it. Come on, then.' The guard waved them through. 'He's asked after you a few times.'

Strolling up a narrow pebble path flanked by tall hedgerows, Keyan shuffled her pipe between her hands in search of a pebble big enough to dribble. A few sure turns brought them to a wide, glossy strip of flagstone that cut across a manicured lawn. It led to a white vase-shaped fountain. Behind it rose a grainy and white haveli. Its segmented roofs were topped in rich terracotta tiles, and its grand windows were unevenly frosted to look like uncut gems. To the back, two minarets with conical heads stood sentinel over the structure.

Keyan stepped off the flagstone and led Zarene around the haveli to a side door. As Zarene made to follow her inside, Keyan spun around and blocked the way with her arms.

'Garden's that way,' she pointed behind the haveli. 'Just keep walking straight ahead. It's nice. I'll come find you, yeah?'

Raising a sceptical brow at her, Zarene gave her half a nod and did as she was told. Slowly.

The servants didn't seem to care that a stranger was roaming the grounds. Some of them greeted her with a tilt of the head. Most stayed focused on the work at hand. Bypassing the enclosure for the kitchens and servants' quarters, then the minarets, Zarene had to climb a slight rise to see the flower garden. It was lovely to behold—far neater than her gardens at Mani Kot and housing a greater variety of flora.

Patting her still-reeling stomach, she walked along the ridge of the rise and settled down under the shade of a rain tree. She removed her turban and the bodkins pinning her braid to the crown of her head. The light breeze sweeping over the grounds cooled her head. Leaning against the tree trunk, stretching her legs out in front, she let the view below lull her into tranquillity.

The haveli's minarets slashed dark shadows across the vibrant garden. A gardener who had been squatting by a flowerbed rose to his feet and deposited his tools and watering can into a wheelbarrow. He then pushed the wheelbarrow through a skewed, conical shadow. Zarene tilted her head, her gaze glued to a dark blot perched on the cone's summit. Scrambling to her feet, she shuffled to one side and shaded her eyes with her hand for a better look.

It was a figure of an elephant standing on its hind legs with its trunk curved up.

Circling the tree, she looked at the shadow's pair—another elephant in the same pose.

A stampede of elephants. A yawning chasm with step-lined walls.

Zarene was sure she'd gone mad this time.

But the ghagra hadn't revealed a new panel, and Reshumnagar hadn't given her what she was looking for. Not yet. This couldn't have been a coincidence. What if the elephants were pointing to a stepwell?

She tried to decipher which way the elephant trunks' shadow pointed using the sun's position. East. But not due east. Maybe a little to the north. How north? She needed a better vantage. From the top of the minaret, for instance.

Her fingers were trembling too violently to pin her braid back up. She tucked her turban and belongings under her arm and hurried down the rise to the eastern minaret. Circling it in search of an entrance, she crashed into an elderly man.

'Creator save us!' he cried, reeling away, a hand clasping his chest. He had on a stiff, cylindrical, black and gold cap, and a grey-brown beard that ran down to his chest—the estate's cleric.

'Chacha, I'm so sorry. Are you all right?'

'Quite all right. Quite all right. Sahiba—' His cheeks turned red upon a hurried assessment of her and her belongings. 'The sahiba has lost her way,' he said with a resigned sigh, extending an arm towards the haveli. 'Come.'

'Actually I—'

'That is the cleric's tower, Sahiba. A place for pious and *righteous* affairs.'

Zarene wrinkled her nose at his implication. Still, left without much of a choice, she followed him to the side door Keyan used, through the servants' passages into the haveli main.

The inside of Polki Ghar seemed larger than it actually was. Curved mirrors were embedded in all its walls and ceilings. Zarene felt like she had entered the inside of a diamond, and imagined it would have been exquisite to behold in candlelight.

From the main foyer, the cleric led her up a grand, curved staircase to the haveli's west wing. At the very end of the corridor, he motioned her through a draped ebony archway into a chamber that glowed an intriguing black.

'If I may, Sahiba,' he said as Zarene was about to enter. 'I'm in no position to stop my master from indulging in excesses, but it's still in my interest to uphold his good name. And for that, I request you to exercise discretion in the future.'

Zarene baulked. The cleric excused himself with a bow and left before she could demand a clarification.

The chamber through the arch had a mirror inlaid ceiling like the rest of the house. To the right, a trio of archways led out to a sprawling marble balcony. The wall to the left was painted a blackish grey that glistened onyx in the afternoon sun's light; bolts of golden lightning streaked the top, and shadowy trees twined with snakes stood scattered beneath. Interspersed between them were divinely painted women, their midriffs bare, their chests bosomy, and their limbs bent and curved in enticing arrangements.

The cleric's unsolicited wisdom made sense now. She had to leave at once. But standing there, in her shapeless qaba, with her wide, unfeminine jaw, she could not help but lament. No one would ever think her so beautiful. No one would find it attractive if she did something as mundane as retreive an unhooked anklet from a forest floor. No, her actions were all ugly. The only thing attractive about her was her dowry, and that would have made a very dull mural.

There were eight women in all, a wide alcove dividing them into two groups of four. Gauzy drapes were hooked to the sides of the alcove, revealing a low, downy and starched bed decorated with silken cushions. Warmth blossomed in the depths of Zarene's stomach upon noticing a tray holding vials of scented oils on the flat-topped chest beside it. A scarf of midnight blue satin sagged out from the chest's clamped lips.

Heat crept up her ears and cheeks. Nose turned up, Zarene swivelled around to escape through the balcony. But a flash of mulberry made her stop. At the far end of the chamber, over a divan, swathed in the shadow of its adjacent wall, was another mural.

It was of three women astride camels, offering each other bouquets of flowers. But unlike the eight women to the left, they did not possess any dainty feminine wiles. They were covered from neck to toe and looked perhaps three times larger than their camels. And their skin was mulberry instead of brown.

They did not look like the figure in her dreams. Nor did they precisely resemble the giantess on the ghagra. But the purple hue of their skin tickled Zarene's senses.

'Maimoona Sahiba, I take it.'

Zarene's answering yelp echoed through the chamber. A man approached her in long, quiet strides. *Stupid cloth slippers.* His grey kurta—raw cotton by its looks, thank Creator—which fastened over his right breast and cinched at the waist, hugged a lean, sinewy figure, and flashed slivers of skin between fastenings. Defined collarbones peeked out from its wide, round collar.

'No—I mean, yes,' she stammered.

'Wildan Palmyr,' he said, raising a cupped palm to his forehead in greeting. His wavy, shoulder-length hair had been coiffed in layers, puffed at the top and fanned out by the ears. 'I am the lord of Polki Ghar. Please allow me to extend my apologies on behalf of Master Hamah. I should've made it known that I hadn't sent for entertainment tonight.'

His eyes, framed by infuriatingly long lashes and lined with kohl, flickered with a playful glint. *How dare Creator give a man lashes so long?* His brows were shaped like two sickles, their upturned blades pointed at each other over the bridge of his nose. They made him look like he was on the verge of either making a naive proclamation or laughing at a silly joke of his own telling.

Zarene cleared her throat to make her indignation known. And to grease her throat. 'Yes, accepted. Only, how did you ...?'

'Keyan,' Palmyr smiled. A dimple appeared on his right cheek. 'I'd asked him why he was so late in collecting his payment. Said he was perfectly charmed by your mela. That you'd even offered him lodging at Mani Kot. And a job.'

'That's right.' Zarene fought the urge to retreat even though he kept a respectable distance between them. 'I did offer h-him a job. One that matched your *alleged* reward.'

His sickled brows drew together over the bridge of his nose. 'I'm a man of my word, Sahiba. The boy's been paid in full.'

'Twenty gold daulatis?'

'Yes.'

'Good Creator, what did you have he-him do?'

'A trifling family dispute that needed settling.' He motioned to the divan. 'Please, have a seat. The refreshments should be on their way.'

Zarene still felt he was too close. 'Thank you, but I shouldn't.'

'Forgive me,' he said, stiffening. 'Let me show you to a proper sitting room.'

'No, that's not it.' Chewing on the inside of her cheeks, Zarene struggled to remember why she had ended up in this indecent chamber in the first place. After what seemed an eternity, she pointed to the mural over the divan. 'Do you know who they are?'

'Who, the howree?'

Zarene gave him a blank look.

'Why, they're the ethereal wives. The definitive prizes of paradise. Creator's most beautiful creations promised to every righteous man at the gates of paradise.' The dimple in his right cheek appeared again. 'You've really never heard of them?'

'I was raised by a Pajcathi nursemaid. Besides, women don't need to be bribed with magical wives to guard their honour.' She matched her pointed look with a wry smile, then shook her head. 'I only ask because of this.'

She shook the ghagra free of the new fabrics and her turban, and splayed it on the divan so to show Palmyr the plum giantess.

'Lovely.' He knelt on the floor to study the needlework and weave. 'A Reshumi purchase?'

'I had hoped. But I haven't had any luck in finding its maker.'

'Yes,' Palmyr mused, running a well-groomed hand down each layer.

The levity in his manner vanished. He withdrew his hand, slid away from the divan, and sat pensively with his arms slung over his knees. Feeling awkward towering over him, Zarene took a seat on the floor as well.

'There's something not entirely natural ...' he murmured. 'How is it you came upon it?'

Sharbat and snacks arrived as Zarene recounted the events of her wedding day. Something in Palmyr's easy demeanour spurred her to give him all the details—about being gifted the ensemble, going to the mehfil, then Tumpa almost clawing the dress off of her in public. She even told him about her ghastly run-in with the late Shurram, eliciting a chuckle of solidarity.

Her bites and sips of the refreshments became incessant as she broached the appearance of the last panel. Palmyr's posture was still easy, his head tilted as he listened. But his eyes grew grave. They reminded her of Naksh. Of Dai Ma. Of her father pacing the pillared study hall. Would he understand? It wasn't worth the risk. She told him what she had told Keyan, instead: the ghagra needed to be destroyed to save Tumpa.

He whistled long and low when she finished, then sighed. 'For what it's worth, I've met the prince of Shandrabad a few times, and you're better off not being his wife.'

Zarene's lips parted in half a gasp, half a smile. She had toyed with the sentiment every now and then, but she couldn't just shrug off the humiliation she'd been dealt.

'I-I may have a lead,' she said, straightening her posture and clasping her palms together. 'To the maker, that is. A stepwell to the east. It'll be mostly dry. That's actually why your Master Hamah found me trying to climb the minaret—to get a look.'

'A stepwell to the east?' The curve of one of his sickled brows bumped up. 'But there aren't any stepwells of note to the east. They're all to the western border where the droughts persist longer.'

'If I could just—'

'No, no, I'll take you upstairs myself, by all means. But trust me, I'd know. My livelihood depends on well-irrigated land.'

He rose to look at the ghagra again from a fair distance. Boyishly balancing his weight on one foot, he flipped a part of the ghagra's ridge to follow the narrative, to follow the party of hunters as they captured the giantess's scion and made a shrine of her. He let go of it with an agitated click of the tongue, and combed his fingers through the fan of hair over his ear.

'What? What is it?'

'It's just that … all this talk of the howree reminds me of an old minstrel's tale. You wouldn't happen to know of Balrakhan the Blessed, would you?'

Zarene shook her head.

'He was the lord of Kua Kot in Pusch Hadd.'

'The abandoned city west of Kandh-i-Arvan?' Her father's trade maps flashed through her mind. Exactly northwest of where they were now.

Nodding, Palmyr continued. 'The story has it that his hakim and wife were lovers, and that the two hatched a scheme to cripple him with poison. Balrakhan's faith in his hakim's abilities waned with each day his malady persisted, so he decided to go to Kandh-i-Arvan to consult with someone more experienced.

'His hakim accompanied him, of course, and made sure his heart gave out before they arrived at Kandh-i-Arvan. He stripped Balrakhan of his lordly attire and dumped his body into the Chanderi, telling everyone that their lord had left camp for a stroll and never returned.

'Exactly a year after, Balrakhan returned to Kua Kot, alive and unscathed. He was accompanied by a howr he claimed was his wife—a gift given to him by Creator, he said, to compensate for the treachery he suffered at the hands of his first wife and hakim. He then dragged his traitors to the city square, and had them whipped and beheaded.

'He lived a prosperous life in the years that followed. His howr wife conjured up a great deal of wealth for him to spend as he pleased. While he gave much of it away in charity, he did nothing of value. No farming, no husbandry, no trade. All because he was convinced he'd never see an end to his wealth.

'But then one day, the howr disappeared. Balrakhan went mad with worry. When he could not find her, he began hunting for another like her. His sons and their sons after them continued the tradition, preying on innocent women, terrorizing all of Pusch Hadd and its neighbouring lands.

'One of these girls was the daughter of a powerful shaman. He was infuriated by his daughter's capture, and cursed all of Pusch Hadd with an eternal drought. Wells and the Chanderi itself began to run dry. The city could no longer sustain life. Almost everyone left. Everyone except the Zulquars. They were that convinced, the fools. Convinced their blood was sacred. That it'd help them find another howr for a wife. And that when that happened, the glory of Balrakhan the Blessed would be restored once more.'

'I thought the wells in Pusch Hadd ran dry because there were too many people living in too small an area,' Zarene said, sceptically. 'The water was being pulled faster than it was being replenished.'

'Logic seems an odd choice for someone speaking of ghagras sprouting panels and driving princesses mad. But like I said, an old minstrel's tale. Come, if it is east you wish to look, we'll have to hurry before we lose the light.'

Master Hamah stirred from his afternoon slumber as Zarene, her lungs and legs burning from the climb, followed Palmyr into the chamber at the top of the eastern minaret. Shooting her a discreetly reproachful look, the old man made to push himself off his cot.

'At ease.' Palmyr waved his hand. 'Do you have a looking glass up here, old man?'

'Yes, Janab. There, Janab.' He motioned to a shelf.

'Good. We won't be long.' He smiled genially before stepping out over the raised threshold, onto the balcony.

Zarene thought to smile at him too, but refrained. Tightening her arm around the ghagra and her fabric, she followed Palmyr out.

The sun was a crisp afternoon gold behind them. The expanse ahead shone like a swath of raw green silk, roughly detailed with sparse knots of black and red, then heavy, busy patches of gold, bronze and copper work. Zarene shut her eyes to the wind's steady caresses of her face as it whipped strands of her hair everywhere. Her stomach ballooned as she sucked in the clean air that faintly smelt of earth.

When she opened her eyes again, the gold illuminating the grounds was a shade darker. Palmyr, his back leaning against the balcony's barrier, hastily averted his eyes from her, wearing a bashful smile he tried hard to suppress. He offered her the looking glass. Tearing her gaze away from how his hair fluttered about his face, she snatched the contraption and aligned the small end against her eye.

'Anything?' he asked.

She couldn't get her eyes to focus. Deep down, she knew she did not have to. 'You don't think …' She lowered the glass, only to be utterly flustered at the sight of his collarbones.

'Think what?'

'You don't think the ghagra was made in Pusch Hadd, do you?'

'It might have been. Far stranger things are said to have happened there. I just thought since you were looking for a stepwell, mostly dry …'

'But a city could have any number of those.'

Though he chuckled, his brows drew together in study of her. 'I fail to see why that'd be a problem. Unless you think your weaver's burrowed into one.'

'No, you're right.' Zarene chewed the inside of her cheek. Her palms grew clammy. She felt like a swollen vein about to burst from the damning truths of her passions and intent. Glancing at the vastness before her, then inside at the weary cleric, she said, 'I have to go.'

Palmyr slouched as he pushed his weight off the barrier. 'They always do,' he murmured into the wind.

He trailed after Zarene as she descended the minaret's steep, spiralling steps.

'Allow me to assign you a few escorts,' he said, keeping up with her brisk pace with hurried, uneven strides.

They crossed the lawns along the side of the haveli.

'Oh, thank you, but I already have my own.'

'Then a word of caution, if I may.' He halted. The solemnity in his words compelled Zarene to do the same. 'I understand you must do what you must for your homeland, but the tradition of hunting howree is still upheld at Pusch Hadd. It wouldn't be wise for a beautiful woman to cross paths with a Zulquar.'

Zarene's breath hitched. 'Creator be with you, Palmyr Sahb,' she said. 'I'll be sure to remember your words of wisdom, along with the kindness you've shown me.'

Before he could reply, she broke into a near sprint to the front lawn. She found Keyan lounging by the vase-shaped fountain, tossing pebbles in the air with the spout of her pipe.

'Pusch Hadd?' Keyan baulked.

'Mhm,' Zarene hummed. She hadn't yet succeeded in shaking Palmyr's aura, his attentiveness most of all, from her consciousness. She dipped a brass pen into the inkpot and mulled words over in her head. 'You're going to accompany the rider I'm sending to Mani Kot with this letter. Dai Ma will pay you the rest of what you're due.'

'And leave you alone? Oh, no. No, no, no, no, no.'

'Keyan, you've upheld your end of the bargain.'

'The garghi's still sitting in your bundle, no?'

Zarene scratched at the engravings on the pen. 'That's not your concern.'

'Well, I'm not going anywhere 'til it's shredded and gone, and that's that.'

'Why?' Zarene snapped, slamming her hand on the writing tray over her lap, nearly overturning the inkpot.

'What's that mean, why?'

'Why do you care so much if it's destroyed or not?'

Keyan's aligned features twisted out of place. Red patches appeared on her cheeks, and her chest swelled with a tirade building inside. 'Because it's evil, is what! And whoever brought it into the world deserves their face beat in!'

Smacking the nearest wall with her pipe, Keyan stormed out. Zarene stared after her, speechless.

SEVEN

2nd Ausihn, 946
Esteemed Abba,

I'd looked forward to welcoming you home myself. However, an urgent matter compels me to send you this letter in compensation for a duty regretfully unfulfilled.

I can imagine your displeasure at my absence. Please know that Dai Ma and my foster sisters did everything in their power to dissuade me from leaving. Also be assured that you have raised a daughter well acquainted with the world. I have taken all necessary measures to keep myself and our men safe, and intend to continue putting your wisdom to good use.

By Creator's grace, I am in good health. I have met with several of your friends on my journey, and look forward to telling you about their tidings when we are together again. I am on my way to Pusch Hadd from Reshumnagar. It is my hope that I will be a better person, one more worthy of being your daughter, by journey's end.

Creator protect you from all ills,

Your loving daughter,
Zarene

The road bending into Pusch Hadd, though amply trodden, was fringed with ruin. Fissures, some as thin as veins, some wide as canals; split segments of the baked dirt road; and mangled structures as far as the eye could see. Clay homes had been razed to rubble, stairs ascended to nothing, and mighty columns lay piled, broken and defeated. There had indeed been a protracted drought that drove the people of Pusch Hadd east, but the city was not abandoned for good until the earthquake of 858.

Zarene's men were wary of coming to Pusch Hadd. There were rumours that it was a haven for outlaws—low lives who would not think twice before slitting a neck for a morsel of bread. Pusch Hadd was also much removed from any major trade route, depriving Zarene of the luxury of accommodations in the homes of her father's acquaintances. They now spent their nights at serais, or in their own tents, and purchased food in bulk. A sturdy mule had to be bought to carry all their supplies.

They had the occasional wayfarer, bullock cart or caravan for company. Zarene, walking alongside Keyan now at all times, never drew more attention than the common wayfaring man, but the uneasiness that took root at Surjalok Chowk still troubled her. Out of the corner of her eye, she occasionally spotted dark shadows lurking by the roadside. They were always gone when she turned to look.

Curving to the right in one broad stroke, the road's inner curve was padded in dusty, coarse, red and yellow-green shrubs and stunted trees. The outer curve was laden with dirt. A settlement of compact, hastily erected mud hovels stood clustered together, just far enough from the thoroughfare.

Women dressed in dark colours filed into their homes, balancing large water pots on their heads. Their figures were rickety but sinewy, and their faces withered to a permanent grimace. Zarene picked up her pace the instant she sensed she and her companions had become the object of their scrutiny.

Further up the bend, embedded in the sea of shrubs, a great wall of sandstone came into view. Though not as high, it resembled the outer wall of the Shandrabad Fort in design. A tributary of dirt broke off from the road, granting unobstructed passage to the women filing in and out to get water. Ordering her bearers to stay outside with the palanquin and mule, Zarene took Keyan and a guard inside.

The wall's numerous archways opened up to an embowered walkway, which flanked a massive square-shaped gorge. Zarene held her breath as she approached the railing and peered over the edge. An awestruck gasp escaped her. Nothing, not even her most vivid dreams, compared to the sheer scale of the stepwell.

As a structure, it must have spanned the same area as all of Mani Kot, running twelve floors deep. A great crack ran down and across the northern stepped wall. It encroached on what could only have been a lavish getaway house protruding from the eastern wall. Flight upon flight of parallel steps led the way down, slanting one way to the landing below, then the opposite direction to the next. Shallow water glimmered in the cavernous tank at the bottom.

Bouncing on her feet, nearly squealing with delight, Zarene beckoned Keyan and the guard to the nearest flight of stairs and skipped downstairs. Only at the first landing did she pause to take stock of her surroundings. There were people about the stepwell collecting water, not just women but men as well. They dotted the steps further down. Like the women, the men were withered but hardened and they made no attempt to hide how they leered. Then again, able-bodied men lounging about in broad daylight never put anyone at ease.

Fragments of their conversations bounced off the walls like the otherworldly calls of ghouls, far away but close as a pulse through the blood. Gulping hard to keep the pounding in her chest at bay, Zarene remembered the incessant whispers with which the orna filled her ears when whispers first obtained it. It seemed like a lifetime ago. She pushed the sounds to a back chamber in her mind and mapped out a descent that steered clear of the Puschis.

The air cooled the lower they climbed. Zarene's skin sang out in relief as her kameez relinquished its sticky hold on her skin. Though the getaway house was three floors high, it could only be entered from its bottom floor porch on the stepwell's second-to-last landing. It looked grand enough to house *something* out of the ordinary. Another mural of the howree, perhaps. Or a special loom if Zarene was lucky.

The eastern wall was the only side clear of loiterers. *Is that a good sign or an ominous one?* Zarene could not decide. Keyan, on the other hand, made her stance clear by blocking the house's entrance with her pipe. 'This isn't a good idea.'

Leaning over the pipe, Zarene softly called into the dim interior, 'Hello?'

They listened to the fading echo of her voice. No answer. No need for further deliberation.

Keyan shook her head. 'It's not safe, trapping yourself in a closed space like that with all these men seeing you going in.'

'Agreed.' Zarene ordered her guard to stand watch outside, brushed the pipe aside and entered.

The thick, smoky saccharine scent of hookah vapours filled the air. Zarene could have sworn she heard a dull gurgle mingle with the low *splish splosh* of water and chatter outside. The entrance and latticed walls permitted ample light into the house, but the shadows its thick columns cast were large enough to make Keyan tighten her grip on her pipe.

'Do you know what you're looking for?'

Zarene's mind conjured up the image of a dark, dying grove. 'I'll know when I see it.'

They passed through an archway into another chamber, this one with little to no light. Keyan tensed. She hooked the spout of her pipe on Zarene's shoulder to make her stop. Zarene flicked it off with an irritated cluck of her tongue, held out her arms before her and kept walking.

She came up against a wall.

'Stairs,' she said. 'We should check if there's anything upstairs.'

'You won't find it here,' a man's voice boomed.

Zarene froze. Behind her, she heard Keyan's pipe whirring through the air as Keyan raised it at the ready.

There was a faint glow of burning coal behind the silhouette of a column Zarene hadn't noticed before. From it appeared a single flame on a stick of pinewood, raised to light the face of the voice's owner.

'Stand back!' Keyan shielded Zarene and pushed her towards the archway with her free hand.

'You're a brave young man, but rest assured I mean you no harm. Please, you'll feel at ease once we've been introduced in daylight.'

❋

The man was elderly, perhaps a few years older than Abba. He had a warm air about him—soft around the edges, a rosy complexion, a salt-and-pepper flecked moustache, and a genuine smile that reached his eyes. He walked out onto the porch with a slight limp and a hand nursing the small of his back. His kurta and pajamas were worn out but immaculately clean.

'I had considered staying invisible,' he chuckled. 'But then that would've been untoward. Azeem Zulquar, at your service.'

He attempted a bow, flinched in pain, and straightened with a silent apology.

'Zarene Maimoona.' She felt a pang of guilt for keeping him on his feet. 'And this here is—'

'Her cousin,' Keyan cut in.

'Ah, so important to have a reliable young man in the family, that too on a journey like yours. Are you on your way to or returning from Akavah?'

Akavah was the holy city far west where pilgrims travelled to pay their respects to Creator.

'Do you receive a lot of pilgrims at Pusch Hadd?'

'Why, of course! I used to be baffled with it myself when I was banished here in my youth. It's so far out of the way. But I suppose there's nothing quite like the draw of legend and conspiracy. Everyone wants to see the splendour of Balrakhan the Blessed with their own eyes. Ha, imagine their disappointment. Still, there is this well and the vault, of course.'

'The vault?'

'Why, yes. There it is, right there.' He pointed at an enclosed guard post embedded in the southern wall. 'You are familiar with the legend of my ancestor, Balrakhan, yes? Well, after the disappearance of my great-great-great-if not even greater grandmother, it is said her sons and their sons captured others like her.'

He spoke over his shoulder as he traversed the landing south. The few Puschis in his way cleared out, their leers glued firmly on them as they passed.

'To keep them from escaping, legend has it my ancestors used their blood powers to construct a special vault.'

At the post's threshold, he let out a weary sigh and motioned inside to a barren chamber with the outline of a petal-domed door etched into its inner-most wall.

'But … there's nothing here,' Zarene nearly whined.

'Legend.' Zulquar's smile belonged to someone who'd told the same silly story one too many times. 'To think, out of all the things our howr blood allowed us to do, we chose to conjure enchantments to lock innocent women away in secret cells for eternity. Always at the stroke of midnight, armed with nothing but a special candle and our incantations.'

'Why midnight?'

Zulquar burst into laughter, then stopped, wincing in pain. 'My dear, you'll have to ask the drunken minstrel who conceived the tale.' His hands returned to his back again. 'For a lonely man like me, it's but the easiest way to make new friends.'

Wincing at Zulquar's obvious pain, Zarene extended her hands in a silent offer of assistance. 'Zulquar Sahb, you should lie down.'

'Oh, it's nothing, nothing. I've lived with it for years. Come, you'll be in want of lodging and a decent meal after your journey. I can't offer much, but I insist you remain at Kua Kot—my home—during your stay here.'

'That's very kind of you, Sahb, but I couldn't impose.'

'Nonsense,' he said with a wave of the hand. 'You'll have plenty of opportunities to use your wagons and horses in the days to come. Come, I beg you not to rob an old man of his sleep tonight. Surely you've noticed the sort of folk that wander these parts. As their best and only link to the outside world,

I'm immune to their unsavoury behaviour, but the same can't be said for you.'

'Cousin'—Keyan gave Zarene's arm a discreet, nearing painful squeeze—'we've got the men to think of, though.'

'Ever the protector,' Zulquar remarked, a twinkle in his eye. 'Don't worry, young man. The house may be undermanned, but your men will be housed and fed to the best of our abilities. You have my word.'

❋

Zarene and her retinue had unknowingly passed Kua Kot while entering Pusch Hadd. Concealed from the main road by a steep rocky rise, its grounds lay south of the stepwell, through a vast stretch of prickly succulents, shrubs, and rock plants, whose vibrant colours were dulled by layers of dust.

Chunks of the estate's boundary wall lay crumbled, leaving wide gaps between towering segments of sandstone. In too much pain to walk all the way to a gate, Zulquar entered his dominion by stepping over a low heap of rubble.

'You'll have to excuse the state of affairs, my friends,' he said, leading them through an outer courtyard swallowed by weeds, dead and alive. Rodents scuffled across the cracked stone floors. Somewhere there was a rustle of twigs, followed by a hiss and a rattle. 'Kua Kot has been in shambles since Destroyer ravaged the land. I've entreated my father and brothers to send help on several occasions, but they see no value in restoring the estate.

'"Well," I say, "if that's the case, release me from my duties as its warden." But that they won't accept. "A Zulquar must always remain at Kua Kot," they say, but really it's to keep my father's lands in the west intact. Do you have brothers, Sahiba?'

Zarene shook her head.

'Ah, all the better. I've got five. You know the way it is—the first son inherits the land, the second becomes a soldier, the third a scholar of theology, then a hakim, then an architect and so on. In my family, the runt becomes warden of Kua Kot.'

Supporting his lower back with both hands now, he led them through the battered reception hall to an inner court. A man in a stiff cylindrical hat, his back crooked with age, sat snipping at the growth that had crept indoors through windows and crannies in the stone.

'This is Master Qawli,' Zulquar said in passing. 'Kua Kot's very own cleric, gardener and sweeper.'

'Creator bless you,' the old man said, raising palm to forehead.

A prayer house lay to one side of the court. From it rose a dangerously lopsided minaret.

'Don't worry yourself, Sahiba. Our Master Qawli doesn't go up there. See?' Zulquar pointed at some scaffolding to its side that was topped with a sturdy platform. 'He makes his calls to prayer from there.'

The living quarters were through the next passage: a newer but plain, block-shaped, grey building surrounded by the older, partially razed structure. It was three floors high and had a terrace furnished with a thick leather awning and a wicker divan underneath.

Inside, Zulquar ordered a maidservant to show Zarene and Keyan to the guest rooms, while he sorted out dinner with the cook. The woman took Zarene's strapped bundle without looking up at her master or the guests, and led them up a narrow staircase to the second floor.

Through the first door on the landing, Zarene caught a brief glimpse of a rustic work table scattered with sheets of parchment, ink and paint pots, tufts of coloured cotton, a bowl of murky water, and a jar holding brushes of varying sizes. Warm familiarity rippled through Zarene as she reluctantly trailed behind the woman. This place was the farthest she could be from Mani Kot—both in distance and appearance—and yet, she felt at ease. Like she was home.

Zarene and Keyan were given adjoining rooms connected by a draped archway. Keyan refused to leave her unattended after the maid took her leave.

'What's gotten into you?' Zarene asked, more than a little irritated. She slid her bundle into the freshly dusted armoire, then pulled her turban off and unpinned her braid.

'What's the matter with *you?* You can't be saying yes to every man that offers you a room!'

'Oh, so you'd rather camp outside with those brigands roaming about?'

'What makes you so sure Zulquar's not one too?'

'Have you *seen* him?'

'He said he's been banished. And did you see the way those men moved out of his way like that? It's not easy, holding power over men like that.'

Zarene's retort remained unspoken. The maid had returned without a sound, carrying two large buckets of water. She deposited them in the wash closet and left.

Sighing, Zarene shrugged out of her qaba and stepped out of her salwar. 'Look, we don't know how long it's going to take to find the ghagra's maker. Isn't it just logical to have a roof over our heads while we look?'

Keyan's eyes burnt into her as she made to pull her kameez off.

'What?' Zarene snapped. 'You need to watch me bathe now too?'

Striking one of the bedposts with her pipe, Keyan stalked off to her chamber and plopped down on the bed. She was still sitting there, stamping the pipe's spout into the floor when Zarene finished bathing. Zarene wondered if she should tell her to take her turban off. The heat had likely gotten to her head. Deciding against it, she pulled the ghagra and orna from her bundle in the armoire and settled herself on the bed to check them for anything new. A new panel still hadn't appeared.

She lay down and drifted into her usual dream: falling down the stepwell, the far-off chime of a call to prayer melding with the wind flapping at her ears. Deeper she fell, but she never reached the bottom, and the usual tug to the heavens never came.

Instead, she woke to Master Qawli's jarringly discordant call to prayer, and the muffled sound of splashing water. The latter came from the wash closet in Keyan's room. The girl had finally come to her senses.

Zarene ached all over. Months of travel had done little to harden her. It didn't matter that she'd just slept on an actual bed instead of a bedroll; her muscles simply refused to accept any bedding that wasn't her soft, downy mattress at Mani Kot.

Cracking her neck and stretching her back, she took a turn about her room before strolling through the arch into Keyan's. To Zarene's chagrin, Keyan's dirty clothes were scattered across the clean bed-linen, her shoes kicked off haphazardly. Her pipe stood propped against the dresser, while her unspooled turban sat on top of it. Zarene started tidying up.

She found the purse holding the ten gold daulatis she had paid Keyan, and another drawstring purse of rough silk nestled under the dirty clothes. A garish ring clasped the second purse's string closure—a silver band with a turquoise stone, marked at the centre with purple swirls.

'Didi.'

Zarene jumped out of her skin. The maid had appeared at the door.

'Dinner is ready, Didi,' she said, then left.

Tossing Keyan's dirty clothes over the purses, Zarene scurried towards the staircase. She halted at the room with the work table. It was empty. Freshly used brushes sat in a bowl of murky water. On the parchment beside them was an incomplete miniature of the Tree of Life. Golden calligraphy and floral patterns ran along its borders. The tree itself was a marvel of abundant skill and patience.

Zarene grinned from ear to ear, studying the other miniatures hanging from clotheslines strung across the room. Among the sketchbooks and scraps were books—pages and pages of miniatures and illuminated texts by the same hand.

'Did you find the rooms to your liking, dear girl?'

'Oh!' Zarene stumbled away from the work table with a surprised gasp. Laughing, she said, 'You've got to stop doing that.'

'Apologies, apologies.' Zulquar entered through what looked like the door of a storage closet at the corner of the room. Hobbling to the work table, he set down a bolt of fresh parchment and an inkpot. 'You like?'

'They're beautiful.' Zarene could not contain her smile. 'How long did it take you to make all these?'

'Oh dear, I can't say I remember. My very first memories are of painting the floors of the ladies' court of my family home back in Kawalthand. It was all I ever wanted to do.'

'But you must have apprenticed under a great master.'

'Yes, yes, and I ran away from home to do it. Fourteen years of age I was, I believe. A father like mine didn't want a miniaturist for a son, you see. A highborn son may dabble in the arts, but to devote oneself to it heart and soul is blasphemy. My father had always been hesitant about which son to make warden of Kua Kot.' He chuckled. 'My decision to run made his decision much easier.'

'Do you regret it, going against his wishes?'

'My girl, I am a lonely fool with no reputation to uphold, no wife to share in my woes and no children to look after.

But every month or so, I complete a piece, and wonder if I could have cherished any of those things had I traded in my soul.'

Zarene pressed her lips together to keep them from trembling. Her vision glazed as she beheld the work room once more. A lifetime's passion fulfilled, but at what cost? She would always have Mani Kot. There was some consolation in that. But her father could not bear to be around her, Dai Ma had made her stance known, and her sisters—foster sisters—had their husbands and children to look after.

Heart aching, she turned her back to Zulquar and pretended to admire whatever it was that was in front of her.

'Ah, you have a keen eye, Sahiba.'

Zarene croaked in confusion. Zulquar stepped around her and unlatched the glass-paned door to a cabinet before her.

'This is indeed what you think it is.'

Her brows furrowed. There was nothing in it besides painted jewellery and spice boxes, and figurines. Zulquar reached to the back and pulled out a fat candle with indented golden spirals snaking around it. Even unlit, it gave off the piquant scent of attar. His hand blackened as he wiped off the dust, and presented it to her for a good look.

'The key to the vault. At least, that's what my uncle, the last warden, told me. Light this at the stroke of midnight, say the blood incantations, and you'll be granted illumination. Ha!'

The breathlessness of being in freefall returned. Zarene felt the wind swiping at her ears, its howls mingling with the hypnotic call to prayer.

Not midnight, her blood thrummed, *but when everyone is at prayer.*

She was not of howr blood, though. Nor did she know any incantations. Her fingers traced the candle's surface for engravings.

'There you are! You scared the life out of me!'

Zarene and Zulquar spun around to find Keyan at the door, leaning on her pipe, one hand on her hip. Though she had left her wet hair down, her obscured form under the oversized chhuba preserved the appearance of a boy.

'No need to be frightened,' Zarene said. 'Zulquar Sahb was kind enough to show me some of his work. And heirlooms.'

To Keyan's bemusement, she waved the candle in the air.

'Oh, it's nowhere near as impressive as yours, young man.' Zulquar smiled at Keyan.

'Mine?'

'Why, that pipe of yours. I've only seen one other in my lifetime. It belonged to a most formidable man. You must be exceptionally talented to inherit yours at such a tender age.'

'It's not like that.'

'But I'm quite—'

'It's just a pipe, is all,' Keyan said, polite but firm.

'Yes, well … I could be mistaken, of course. It was such a long time ago. Come, I believe dinner has been served.'

❋

Dawn. During the morning call to prayer. It was the only time they could attempt anything without drawing unwanted attention.

Dinner was a short affair. The ache in Zulquar's back became more intense just as they were finishing their after-meal teas. He bid them good night and ordered his cook to help him to his chamber on the third floor.

Back in their rooms, Zarene told Keyan to lay beside her so she could share her plan without being overheard by the ghoulish maid who seemed to have the ability to materialize out of thin air.

'I don't know. We could get caught sneaking out, though.' Keyan's straight brows dipped and clinched as she likely ran through the possibilities in her head.

'Then we'll just tell the truth. Zulquar Sahb will get a good laugh from it.'

'You sure this'll work?'

'Now how can a man be certain of such a thing, Sahiba?' Zarene mimicked the shopkeeper from Surjalok Chowk.

They both snorted.

'Anything to find the howree, I guess. It's past time we head home.'

Zarene let out a long breath. They lay silent for a long while, knowing full well neither would sleep a wink that night.

'Can I ask you something?' Zarene asked.

'No.'

'Your pipe … it *did* belong to your father. You told me that yourself. So why'd you get so defensive when Zulquar Sahb brought it up?'

'I wasn't defensive. It just isn't a … a … whatever fancy word he said it was. It's just something of my Baa's I like having on me.'

Another stretch of silence.

'Can I ask you something else?'

'Ugh,' Keyan said irritably. 'I'm going to my own bed.'

'No, please, last one, I promise.'

Keyan rolled onto her back and huffed.

'Why did you come with me all this way? Surely it's not because you've grown fond of me. Why do you want to find them, the howree?'

Keyan entwined her fingers across her stomach and shut her eyes. For a moment, Zarene thought she'd fallen asleep.

'Baa was … he was a courier like me,' she finally said. 'When I was ten, he left for a job for a powerful sahb who needed him fetching someone gone hiding in the Tankh forest. An escaped daughter or wife or some such. He was gone near two years. We thought he was as good as dead, but then he came back.

'Only he was different. Nice enough to us chillun, but a rabid dog to Maa. Kept raving she couldn't be the dirt on *her* feet. Kept going on about how she was so lovely as wine and precious as omatusts.'

'Amethysts?'

'Right, that. Nobody knew what he was on about. I only found out 'cause one of Palmyr Sahb's women told me he gifted her some. Gemstones, they are. Purple coloured. Folk like me and Baa, we're as simple as they come. Why'd he know what a bloody omatust is?

'I knew then, someone'd cursed Baa in that forest, yeah. I've been trying to get a job through Tankh ever since, but … it wasn't what's written. When I saw the pitchures on the garghi, I thought, *This is it! This is the closest I'm going to get.*'

'But if there is a howr in the vault, it might not be the same one your father saw.'

'Doesn't matter.'

'What will you do?'

'I'm going to make her destroy the garghi first. Then I'm going to kill her, plain and simple.'

Zarene rolled over with a jerk. Her hand slid up to the left side of her chest where her heart beat a smidgeon faster. Keyan had to be bluffing. Everyone thought of harming others. Very few actually went through with it.

❋

The skies were still dark, but critters and birds had begun stirring outside and in. Pulling on her qaba, Zarene lit a fresh candle and crept down the corridor.

'Keep an eye out for that maid,' she told Keyan before leaving.

She removed her sandals outside the workroom, tiptoed to the cabinet and pulled its door open by its latch. Tucking a few loose strands of hair behind her ear, holding her breath, she stuck her hand in. Her knuckles collided with a figurine; it tilted off balance and straightened with a resounding *tak tak*. Fingers shaking, she threaded her hand deeper and grabbed the candle.

Keyan waited for her in the dark corridor, dressed to be on her way as always. To Zarene's dismay, she had the orna and ghagra tucked under one arm.

'Almost forgot these,' Keyan said in an exasperated tone that reminded Zarene of Dai Ma.

'Right, best be on our way, then.'

The cook, who doubled as the guard, sat fast asleep by the main entrance. Past him, the path to the stepwell was clear. Zarene only worried she could not see what she was stepping on in the dark. She was never one to rely on prayer, but in this one instance, when a snake could bite her at any moment, she made an exception.

Their descent down the stepwell's southern wall to the vault took longer than it had during the day; it would have been foolish to take more than one at a time, considering the disrepair of the structure. By the time they arrived at the guard post, the inkiness of the night sky had given way to a lighter shade of blue.

Standing before the outline of the door within, Zarene lit the indented candle. The intensity of its attar fragrance sent both of them reeling in a fit of coughs. Noses wrinkled, stomachs turning, they waited.

And waited.

'Oho, what if we don't hear him, though? It's getting light out.' Keyan scratched under her turban, then kicked the nearest wall.

She was right. They were too far from Kua Kot, too deep in the ground to hear Master Qawli.

'Damn it,' Zarene hissed.

She flattened her right palm inside the outline. The familiar voices returned again, steady as a strengthening heartbeat. They muffled her ears from hearing anything else. She turned to look at the orna balled under Keyan's arm. It was vibrating with a life of its own.

'What the—' Keyan dropped the clothes and stepped back as one does from a venomous snake.

Pop.

Master Qawli's drawling and discordant call blared in Zarene's ears.

She didn't have to think. The words just tumbled from her lips:

'There is a song they will not hear,
A strain so strange and yet so dear.
Savour it and trust it you must,
Steadfast and certain as solitude and dust.
A bard's song sung may ring empty,
Where silence holds the key to aplenty.'

They stared at the wall, expectantly.

Nothing.

Zarene's heart plummeted. Her face grew hot and her hands clammy; she felt like she'd been sentenced to death by fire.

'It's not opening,' Keyan pestered. 'Didi, why's it not opening?'

'I-I-I-don't know. I don't know what else I can—' Inhaling, she repeated the words again:

'There is a song they will not hear,

A strain so strange and yet so dear.
Savour it and trust it you must,
Steadfast and certain as solitude and dust.
A bard's song sung may ring empty.'

She pressed harder against the wall, imagined her intent as if it was molten liquid and poured it into the wall. Keyan started to say something, but Zarene silenced her, sharply brandishing both candles in the air. Outside, Master Qawli's call drew to a close, and all fell silent.

Beside her, Keyan's shoulders slumped. The wall remained as it was, but Zarene felt it stir deep within. A bolt of iridescent silver shot through the outline, and the stone under Zarene's hand dissolved to nothing. A gust of odorous fumes assaulted their eyes and nostrils as a moaning blackness yawned open before them like the mouth of a whale.

Leaning in headfirst, Zarene raised the candles to gauge the lay of the vault. The indented candle flickered violently at the threshold. It dimmed to a spark upon crossing it. A staggering pain knocked the air from her lungs, crushing her from all sides. Behind her, Keyan cried out in horror. Zarene quickly snatched the candle back. The flame strengthened, and the portal remained open.

'It will have to stay outside.' Zarene set it down with a trembling hand. 'You stand out here. Make sure it doesn't go out.'

She reached for the bundle. The spout of Keyan's pipe came to rest on her hand.

'You finish your binnuch in there, then I finish mine, yeah?'

'Yeah.' Zarene smiled as best as her throbbing ribs allowed.

The one candle in hand, Zarene climbed over the raised threshold. The nauseating smell of rot made her skin crawl. She raised the candle overhead and pivoted slowly—nothing but absolute darkness.

'Hello?' The word echoed long and low before being swallowed by the cavity's hollow moan. She had to go deeper to find the dark, dying grove. On she walked, the *clop clop* echoes of her sandals leading her way. Chills shot up her spine every time the candle's flame flickered. That was good, she told herself. It meant she was nearing the end, to the place where she was meant to be.

She came up against solid metal—a bar. It was one of many. She stuck the candle between two and recoiled.

Bones—entire skeletons—lay heaped within. Many still wore thin gold necklaces, anklets, and rings that had long lost their lustre. The earrings had fallen off and scattered across the floor with the decay of flesh.

Her throat parched, Zarene looked beside the cage to find another. Then another, and another, each filled with the remains of bodies. This was all there was. This atrocity. But how could that be? There had to be some purpose for bringing her here.

'Zarene Didi!' Keyan cried in the distance.

The line of cages curved back towards the portal. Refusing to accept defeat, Zarene tried the bars for a way to get through, to go deeper. Most were unyielding. Some shifted ever so slightly. She was ready to try them all until she found *something*.

'Zarene Didi!' Keyan seemed farther away now.

'Hold on!' Zarene snapped, trying to ignore the skull glaring at her as she gave another bar a jerk.

'He really is a most dutiful protector, your pretend cousin.'

Zarene whipped around, a gasp caught in her throat. Candlelight illuminated Zulquar's fatherly face.

'I've startled you again. My apologies.'

'Zulquar Sahb, I was only just … wait, how did you—'

'Dear girl, I'm descended from howr blood. You may not be the ethereal beauty of legend, but I sensed the lure of your blood right away.'

Instinct made Zarene retreat. 'Zulquar Sahb, I'm looking for the howree just as you are. I'm only a plain dressmaker.' Breaking into a cold sweat, she waved the bunched-up ensemble at him, 'See this? This was made by a howr. I think it's what you—your blood—sensed. It calls to me too. Please, I o-only wish to learn its make.'

A slew of roaring cries poured through the portal, like the angry howls of a storm at sea. Adrift in them came sounds of clashing metal.

'Hear that?' Zulquar edged closer, hands folded behind his back. 'I've told the Puschis to go easy on the Koudabhakt boy, but too long and they *will* kill him.'

He raised one end of the orna and ran it through his fingers. 'I'm not an unreasonable man, Zarene Sahiba. I won't stop you from taking what you came here for. Nor will I ask you to serve as my wife. I only demand the riches I am due for my life's service. It is only what is fair.'

Zarene tugged at the garment. Her chest constricted with fear, and she heaved with a dry sob. 'You have to believe me, if there was something I could do, I would.'

His features almost softened with compassion. Catching her wrist, he twisted her around so her back was flush against him, her neck locked in the crease of his elbow. The candle fell from her hand and went out. Zarene tried to wriggle free. She clawed at his arm with her free hand. When he let go of her wrist, she used both.

A dagger's tip jabbed her side. Zulquar lifted her off her toes and squeezed harder.

'Plea-hease!'

'Gold, diamonds, rubies, royal bonds, I don't care. Just summon it. Summon it like you did the vault.'

He jabbed her side again. He may have broken skin, but she didn't feel it. She only felt the burning clamp in her neck, and the excruciating desperation of a body in collapse.

The halls of Mani Kot appeared before her; her sisters sprawled out in the sitting room before a lavish feast while Dai Ma directed the servers. Her twitching legs carried her through the grounds, which still housed the awnings from the mela. There was Keyan, hanging from the awning's frame, swinging her legs back and forth till she had enough momentum to flip onto the canopy.

'Come now, dear girl. Are you so stupid to let your stubbornness cost you your life?'

Zarene dug her nails into Zulquar's arm. She raised her knees up to her chest and threw her feet up in the air. They crashed to the ground, pulling Zarene into a low squat with a howling Zulquar curled over her. She sidestepped and ducked, freeing her head from his grasp. It was too dark to see where he fell. Coughing to free her windpipe, Zarene bolted towards the light on unsteady legs.

She hopped over the threshold, launched herself at the indented candle, and slammed her palm onto the flame, numb to its burn.

It happened in half a heartbeat: A strained *yah*, a swirl of olive and a *swish* of silver. Outside the guard post, Keyan spun mid-air using her pipe for leverage. She kicked one brawny Puschi wielding a butcher's knife in the jugular, then planted her feet and bowed to drive her pipe into another Puschi attacking her from behind. The pipe's tip was soaked in blood when she yanked it out of him.

Zarene was too stupefied to notice that a thin layer of muslin had slipped underneath her. It jerked her off the ground, almost convincing her this was all a terrible dream. She cried out, petrified, as the orna launched itself through the throng of Puschis with her on it. Once over the water, it tilted in a sharp incline to fly over the wall.

No! Not without Keyan! Turn around! Turn around!

At the boundary wall, the orna flipped over without warning, nearly throwing Zarene off. The fabric was too smooth and her hands were too clammy. Her grasp was tenuous at best. Higher it rose, whizzing circles along the stepwell's boundaries.

Zarene's blurred vision could only make out Keyan's olive chhuba, fluttering in her wake as she fled from her assailants.

The orna slowed when the fight below matched its own trajectory. It descended to the ninth level, far enough behind the Puschis so their attention remained fixed on Keyan. Five unmoving masses lay strewn in swelling pools of blood. Keyan and the Puschis—there were seven—skidded on the blood, their sandals smearing it all over the tenth-level landing.

'Keyan!'

The Puschis whipped around. Keyan skidded to a sloppy halt. She locked eyes with Zarene for a breath before leaping into the air, swiping her pipe across the nearest Puschi's neck, and sprinting away from his collapsing body.

Now.

The orna dove at her, zipping past swinging blades and vengeful cries. Zarene held out her arm. Keyan caught it mid-run and, to Zarene's consternation, tugged down. Zarene braced herself for a crash, but Keyan deftly wrenched her legs onto the soaring orna. Landing in a hunter's crouch, she restored the bloody pipe to her dominant hand.

Its spout was gone. In its place was a slender blade with menacingly crooked kinks towards its tip. Zarene shrank away. Keyan gave her a remorseful look, then turned away and prowled to the orna's back edge to look at the shrinking figures below.

Zarene looked back, too, taking in the shrinking form of Kua Kot.

What are you doing? We have to retrieve my men. We have to go home.

The orna continued, unwavering in its course.

My men. I can't just leave them there. Turn around!

'No, turn around!' Zarene wailed, her voice still grizzly. 'For the love of Creator, turn around!'

She began sobbing. It was no use. Unless she and Keyan wished to jump to their deaths, they would have to go wherever the orna took them.

EIGHT

Cool moisture smacked their faces, then dried off. Their clothes grew heavy with damp as they lifted through sparse clouds into a clear stretch of blue, speeding towards the eastern horizon. Though the sun burnt bright, a sharp chill pierced through their flesh and sank into their bones. Hot tears stung Zarene's eyes; they had little to do with the winds whipping her to a battered mass of flesh and bone. How could this happen? When would things stop being so dour that she'd have to ask herself the same question over and over again?

Vast stretches of rock, woodland, dirt, sand and water slipped under them. For a moment, Zarene wanted to hope they were heading home, but home was farther south. Not due east. They were covering too much ground. It would take weeks, no months to retrace their steps. But how would they even do that? Zarene had left the purse she kept slung around her neck at Kua Kot, and the rest of her money was still hidden in the palanquin.

And her men! The men who'd been nothing but loyal and gracious to her this entire time. The guards were accomplished with their blades, but the bearers were unarmed. They would have been caught unaware, and grossly outnumbered. Her hands were drenched in their blood. And for what?

'Didi?' Keyan shouted over the blustering wind. 'The garghi … you destroyed it, yeah?'

'I don't know. I had to leave it in the vault.'

And the vault was sealed now.

Zarene sat with her back to Keyan, hunched over crossed legs. She could see the pipe's bloody blade from the corner of her eye. Keyan carefully held it over the orna's side so it did not drip blood onto the orna. The thinning air made Zarene lightheaded. Arranging her knees to one side, she grimaced as she twisted her torso to face Keyan.

'We haven't any money to get us home.'

Keyan shook her head with a click of her tongue. She pulled her chhuba open and patted an inner pocket bulging with two lumps. Palmyr's silk purse, fettered by the turquoise ring, peeked out. 'I have Palmyr Sahbji's gold as well as yours. You'll pay me back at Shandrabad, no problem.'

There were, of course, plenty of problems that could arise. They could land up too far from Navaarat, get robbed, or run out of coin before they reached Shandrabad. But, in that moment, none of this ruffled Zarene quite as much as the turquoise ring. She remembered it now, remembered the stubby finger that wore it and the potent smell of chewing tobacco that accompanied it a lifetime ago at Naksh and Tumpa's mehfil.

A momentary rush of clarity dulled the pain of everything else, perhaps even made it a little more bearable. She beheld Keyan's neatly aligned features in a new light.

'What did Palmyr have to gain from killing Laal Shurram?'

Keyan's jaw tightened. Her bottom lip disappeared behind the top. Her eyes were alight, too defensive to truly look at Zarene.

'It's his, isn't it, the ring? You took it from him when you killed him.'

Keyan hugged her knees to her chest and lay her head on them. The top of her turban obscured her face.

Creator, I've been such a fool. Zarene stared at the turban, then at Keyan's thumb absentmindedly rolling the bloody pipe in her palm. *Then again, that wouldn't be a first.*

She'd been so stupid, so desperate to find a kindred spirit that she didn't once find Zulquar's eagerness to divulge his ancestors' lore suspicious. Now, here she was again, in the company of another liar.

She had lied to Keyan too, of course. Not that it mattered anymore. The ghagra and its secrets were lost to her forever.

They continued speeding forth. Peaks of rock dusted with snow rose from the horizon, their edges smudged and soft in the morning light as though they had been drawn on blue canvas with charcoal. The Heemdanga Mountains. Hours must have passed, yet the sun remained fixed before them. The smudged edges solidified, then split into separate formations. Their peaks stretched skyward in all their infallible majesty and blotted out the sun.

The orna descended into the thick of the range. It was uncompromising in its speed, poised to crash into a rock face at any given turn. Zarene and Keyan instinctively crouched low and bunched handfuls of muslin in their fists to keep from toppling over. Zarene's dinner from the night before pushed up her sore throat as the orna swerved, spun, dove down and shot up along the slopes and ridges. Going faster, blindingly so, it chose a mountain and spiralled down and around it.

An impenetrable wall of air pressed up against Zarene's face. Her lungs were desperate for air, but her airways shrank and burnt. The blur of brown, grey, blue, and white around her dimmed to mere shadows sweeping past. Her grasp on the orna loosened. She felt Keyan's slight frame curl around her; long, cold fingers clasped over her arm.

The taut surface of the orna went slack. They fell on hard, uneven ground, bouncing and tumbling downhill until they crashed to a stop in an undignified heap. As Keyan's weight lifted off her, Zarene inhaled a timid breath, afraid it would hurt. It did. But such was the curse of staying alive.

Keyan was already roaming the inclined crest's edge when Zarene sat up. The ground was grassy and the ridges in view were flanked by the tops of evergreens. They were not very high up. Zarene's shoulders tensed up to her ears,. She tightened her qaba around her and hugged herself as she joined Keyan in her study of their surroundings.

'That there's Chilchonchu,' Keyan said, pointing at a peak that curved to one side like an eagle's beak. 'If we follow this ridge around, we can get to the Cho Mu Man Pass in three, maybe four days.'

The Cho Mu Man Pass was the principal thoroughfare connecting Navaarat further north to Xingho. Except during winter months, tens and hundreds of merchant caravans traversed the corridor, hauling entire households and entourages along with their wares. With Keyan's money and Zarene's name, they'd be able to buy safe passage back to Shandrabad. They could even stop by Keyan's hometown, Qokhura, in Barwasi on the way to pay her family a visit.

Zarene's body warmed as they climbed down the slope and followed the ridge towards Chilchonchu through the woodlands. She had tried her best to fashion the orna into a turban, but it was too thin to pad her ears against the chill. The concerted effort it took to keep up with Keyan made it easy to ignore that she had lost all feeling in her feet.

They stopped at a stream shortly after midday and snacked on nuts and berries Keyan had astutely plucked during their hike. Zarene gulped down a handful of freezing water, only to cough it all out. Her throat was still too sore, the water too cold. She tried again, slowly, tears rolling down her cheeks as she forced the searing cold water down.

Downstream, Keyan washed the head of her pipe clean. She wiped it dry with her chhuba's sleeve and sheathed it in the detachable spout. The latch that held the pieces together was indistinguishable on the pipe's surface once it was snapped in place.

She sensed Zarene's eyes on her. 'Baa was a Koudabhakt,' she said in a hushed voice. 'Trained to protect Qokhura in case the Xwaie Emperor comes charging.'

'Until he became an assassin for hire,' Zarene corrected.

'Mountain country's different from Navaarat. Your sultans keep saying they're our friends, but we're forgotten is what we are, plain and simple. We'd never seen a copper from all your trade, never seen the good of all your fair and mighty justice. You don't think our guides helping your caravans cross the Heemdangas are worth more than a few pulses and grains, just enough to keep us living and running for your own convenience. Most of us are lucky to get a goat to milk through winter.'

Keyan heaved a sigh. 'If a Qokhuran like me wants anything better, training as a Koudabhakt's the only way.'

'And you had to take your father's place after what happened in Tankh.'

'No, not like that. Girls can train and all in the monastery, but only till the womb's blood comes, yeah. We're not allowed into the order.' Keyan grimaced. 'Something stupid about keeping our souls pure to save husbands and chillun from the curse. When Baa disappeared, we thought we'd get by till Hiranshu, my little brother, got old enough, but his heart's too gentle. He'd make a real bad Koudabhakt, and I'd not want him dead.'

She fell silent. Zarene should have been afraid to be sitting across from a killer, but she found herself feeling sorry. More than anything, she felt guilty.

'I don't like it, what I do,' Keyan said after a long stretch. 'But what I do, I do quick, without giving too much pain. That's why my heart says it's good work. Honest work.' She pulled the silk purse from her chhuba and wriggled Shurram's ring free. 'This, though … this wasn't part of the deal. I was wrong taking it like that.'

Before Zarene could say anything, she flicked it into the water. The current carried it downstream, out of sight.

'You didn't have to do that.'

'We should keep moving.' Keyan stood up and flapped her hands against her sides. 'We can still cover a fair way before deciding what to do for cover tonight.'

Zarene didn't move. Chewing on the inside of her cheeks, she called after Keyan with a hoarse voice. 'I have to tell you something.'

'Tell me as we walk. Up now. Come, come.'

Shaking her head, Zarene said, 'The ghagra … I don't know if it was the real reason the prince's bride went mad.'

The colour drained from Keyan's face. Her right eye twitched. She took a pronounced step towards Zarene, her head tilted as though she had misheard.

'I … I never wanted to … I thought if I came with you to Reshumnagar, that maybe … that I could find its maker … that they could teach me how to make another.'

A fraught look of disbelief distorted Keyan's neatly aligned features. Deep red splotches appeared on her face. Her fists clenched and her flat chest heaved underneath her chhuba. Zarene drew back, anticipating an outburst, perhaps even a blow.

Keyan bit back her words. Nostrils flared, she whirled around and stormed off.

'Keyan.' Zarene scrambled to her feet and went after her. 'Keyan, wait!'

Keyan swivelled around to look her in the eye. 'How could you be so selfish?'

'At least I'm not a murderer!'

She regretted the words as soon as they had left her mouth.

Keyan's eyes narrowed. She thumbed the pipe up her palm to the ready and prowled towards Zarene's retreating form. 'Chantan, Gilnish, Burmat, Khurkanat, Rajnal, Purba, Malkan—what about them, huh? They're all dead because of you!'

'I didn't mean that.' Zarene struggled to meet Keyan's gaze. 'I'm sorry.'

Wrinkling her nose, Keyan resumed her course. 'You're on your own.'

'Keyan! Keyan, please, I'm sorry. Believe me, if I'd known this would happen, I would never have—'

'Leave me alone.'

'Please, you know that I can't—'

A flash of metal slashed through the air. Zarene jerked her head back, as the pipe's sharp head appeared a hairsbreadth from her neck, its tip pressed against her skin.

'Leave. Me. Alone!'

With a warning glare, Keyan retracted the blade and walked away.

Zarene watched the shadows of the evergreens swallow her. She stood there a long while, too drained to care or carry on.

She tried to conserve the last vestiges of light in the misery ensconcing her. She wanted to go home. It was the only path she had left. Everything could be right again with Dai Ma's counsel. Or even her father's. If she could smell the warm sweetness of the Mani Kot gardens again.

She trudged ahead, the same way as Keyan. The plumes of warm mist engulfing her with every exhale cautioned her to be more miserly with her breaths. A tense ache built up between her shoulder blades. It spread up her neck and down her back and legs. Her teeth chattered no matter how swiftly she moved, or how tightly she wrapped her qaba about her torso. She tried covering her ears with the turban she had made out of the orna. It unfurled, exposing her head to the viselike chill.

In a moment of rage and frustration, Zarene flung the orna to the ground. She stamped on it and kicked it away before resuming course. Fallen leaves skittered over her feet, flowing in the opposite direction. Their rustle—no whispers—raised a tight seal over her ears, shutting out every other sound. Gripped by that all too familiar sensation of being watched, she spun around.

The tide of leaves was carrying the orna to an old, balding tree with scaly bark. Casting a cursory glance at her intended path, Zarene took small, uncertain steps towards it. The orna slithered around the trunk's girth and stopped before a wide triangular hollow carved into it.

The seal over her ears fell away.

'Tsk, tsk, tsk,' a crackling voice sounded, shooting tremors up Zarene's spine.

An arm protruded from the hollow's darkness, mottled grey with a purple hue in places, flaking like the bark sheltering it. It plucked the orna from the forest floor.

'You should take greater care of borrowed clothes, Zarene Maimoona.' Cloaked shoulders and a hooded head followed the arm. 'For what good is an orna without its ghagra?'

The figure raised its head to fix a pair of shrewd, cloudy grey eyes rimmed with sweeping strokes of white on Zarene. Its birdlike features were crowded around a pert but flaking nose. Slicked plumage, the brown of over-dried henna, peered out from under the hood. Wine-coloured sap trickled through the cracks in her thick dark lips, giving the face a velvety gleam.

The hooded scion from the ghagra's panels.

Zarene resisted the urge to recoil. 'I'm sure you can just hatch another one.'

The corner of the scion's lips twitched in amusement. 'That we can, that we can. And you will watch us do it. That is, after all, why you came so far, is it not?'

'My men are dead because of you.'

'A bold accusation, but one we must deny.' The orna snagged against the scion's rough fingers as she folded it. 'For we did everything in our powers to dissuade you.'

'Dissuade me?' Zarene balled her fists, shaking with anger. 'You paraded a poisoned feast before a starving urchin!'

'Tsk, tsk, tsk. Such self-pity is cheap from your mouth, Zarene Maimoona. This poison, it was inside you all along. Us? We tried to rid you of it.

'Think hard. We gave you every choice—the love and loyalty of your homeland, the finest fabrics your land had to offer, a suitor who would have loved you as you are … we even showed you what becomes of obsession gone unchecked. But you kept pushing. We did not feed you the poison, child. You did that yourself.'

Zarene swayed on the balls of her feet. Willing her knees not to buckle, she shook her head. 'No more.'

'No more?' The white rims of the scion's eyes rounded. 'After coming so far?'

'I just want to go home. That's all I want.'

'Of course.' The scion nodded. She tucked the folded orna into her robe, then rummaged through its folds and extracted a bundle of silk.

Zarene gasped in equal measures of dismay and desire. The ghagra. The scion bit off a flake of bark-like skin from the pad of her finger, tapped it on the garment, then sent it unfurling to Zarene's feet.

'Are you certain, child? You have borne a great deal … *lost* … a great deal to get here.'

Zarene's fingers itched to reach out. To learn the secret behind such extraordinary finery. She stopped short of picking it up as the panel depicting her and Keyan strolling through her garden caught her eye. A small wine-coloured stain blotted her figure now, garish and bright next to Keyan's beige tunic.

How could you be so selfish?

No more.

'I'm certain,' Zarene gulped. 'If the ghagra is the cause for Princess Tumpa's ailment, I wish for her to be free of it. I wish for it to … to be destroyed.'

'We understand.'

The scion bowed her head. She swirled in a circular motion the wrist of the hand with the bitten finger, then balled the fingers into a fist and curled into her chest.

The stain on the ghagra spread, consuming Zarene's image, then Keyan's, drenching the delicate fabric in something thick—a red deeper than wine. Bubbles appeared in the sticky wetness and simmered across the surface. The thread disintegrated in growing clumps. Zarene wrinkled her nose at the stench of decay it gave off.

It was all gone in a matter of minutes. Not a trace of the ghagra remained on the forest floor. Zarene stared at the clear patch of dirt it left in its wake; the fluttering leaves erasing all evidence of what had just occurred.

'Your nobility is admirable, child. The princess will now be free and fit to hone her talents.'

Tearing her gaze from the ground, Zarene blinked. 'What?'

'Naksh Manandha's bride, Tumpa. She is a weaver's daughter, did you not know? Before she fell ill, she could make cloth that looked like streams of gold under one light and the summer sky at dusk under another. All with the most meagre of threads. Her hand at embroidery was earning her quite the reputation as well.'

The forest grew denser and taller around Zarene. A gulf of leaves and fallen branches stretched out between her and the scion, whose words rang shrill in Zarene's ears. The chill constricted her insides till it all snapped. A violent blaze of heat flushed through her. She saw nothing but red. A wail fought its way up her throat, but she had no energy left to shed tears.

'Keyan!' Zarene strained her voice to its limit, but there was no sound. She wrenched her rigid feet around to get away. To go home. But her wobbling legs gave out, and she landed on the ground, face first. 'Keyan!'

'You are much too slow, child,' came the scion's voice. 'The Qokhuran won't wait for you. Nobody will.'

Pushing herself back up, Zarene stumbled ahead without looking back. The chilly air numbed her lungs, yet she kept moving, stumbling into trees and boulders in her path.

Follow the ridge around Chilchonchu. Get to the Cho Mu Man Pass. There may still be hope.

Zarene repeated Keyan's words over and over again, until they lost their meaning. Daylight slipped through her numb fingers. By nightfall, she had lost count of how many times she had passed the same mossy tree and mushroom cluster.

She found a tree shielded from the harsh northeastern winds by a copse. Gathering branches of dried fern, she propped them up against its trunk to make a tent. She tried to build a fire, but her hands were too slow and, after a few hours of trying, too bloody. Captive to the ruthless chill, she fared no better than shards of a broken teapot being jostled in a dustpan. There was nothing to do but pile dead ferns over herself and pray to get through the night.

In between listless stretches of unconsciousness, Zarene thought the night wind howled her name. She shuddered at the prospect of going home. Soon, Tumpa would begin flaunting her craftsmanship before all of Shandrabad. And everyone would come running to Mani Kot, masking their spite with courteous conversation. They would ask, 'And what do *you* have to show for all your stubbornness?'

❋

A fit of phlegmy coughs ushered Zarene into the morning. A wall of pain pinned her where she lay. Her blanket of ferns crumbled to dust as the coughs continued to rack her body. Feebly brushing the leaves from her face, she winced at the fresh throbs of pain around her eyes. The early morning light was unbearably bright.

'Zarene Didi?' the heavens echoed.

'Key—' Another fit of coughs ensued.

'Zarene Didi? Lo, lo, lo, Didi!'

A welcome shadow blotted the sunlight. The itchy branches fell away, and a firm hand pulled her upright. Through the haze she made out Keyan's turban and chhuba, though it now looked more grey than olive.

'Hai yo, you're burning up. Why didn't you answer me last night?' Keyan tried to bring her to her senses with light slaps to her cheek. 'You need to stand, come, come. We need to get you to a healer, yeah?'

'The ghagra,' Zarene mumbled as Keyan hauled her to her feet. 'It was waiting in the ho-hollow, and I told tha-that thing to get rid of it. Just like I said I would.'

'Never mind that. I need you to walk. Up, up, now.'

Zarene could barely land a step; her feet were beyond her control. Keyan threw one of Zarene's arms around her neck, grabbed her by the waist, and dragged her. Qokhurans were renowned for their dogged resilience and their skill in carrying heavy loads across the Cho Mu Man Pass. It would take longer than four days to reach the pass now, but Keyan was sure she could get them there eventually.

But as Zarene's senses dimmed in the brightening sun and she grew more fuddled with fever, one thought blared loud and clear: she could not go home.

The failure. The disappointment. The taunts. The judgement. The comparisons. The isolation. She could not endure it. Not again. Not after giving everything she had.

And she didn't have to.

Keyan lugged her a long way, though not as much as she would have liked, before halting for a break. Like the previous day, she gathered an assortment of nuts and berries for their midday meal. Zarene insisted Keyan eat her share. Everything tasted so bitter.

Propped up against a tree, she fought her drooping eyes to watch Keyan pop one nut after the other into her mouth.

'Kehaan.' Her voice was a thin rasp. 'Can I ahsk for a favour?'

'Sure.' Keyan hopped onto her haunches. 'You need to pee?'

'No. Two favours, actually. The first is yo-hor payment. I know I said twenty gold daulahtis, but I don't think Mani Khot's treasurer will be tooh'—she coughed into her shoulder—'too keen to give you the rest of the ten still owed.'

Keyan stood, wheeling her pipe in the air and smashing its spout into the ground. 'Why's that?'

'They won't think it a job done if I don't make it bahck.'

'Oho, but I'll get you back, no?' Keyan's irritation morphed into alarm as she registered Zarene's increasingly vacant eyes.

'That's my second favour. I need you to do what you do best. I need you to do it to me.'

Mouth twisted in disgust, Keyan stared at her long and hard before scooping her back on to her feet. 'The fever's got to your head, that's what.'

'I-I know I haven't money to give you,' Zarene gasped in her ear.

'Money? I wouldn't do it if you gave me all the money in Navaarat.' She jostled Zarene to get her to move her legs. They flopped like dead eels.

'You'll get to the pass faster,' Zarene insisted.

'I'm taking you to Cho Mu Man Pass and that's that.'

As Keyan soldiered on, dragging Zarene's dead weight, Zarene drifted in and out of consciousness. After what seemed like an eternity, Zarene's side and head met with a hard blow. She found herself lying on the ground, looking up at a purplish red sky.

Keyan kneeled beside her, bracing herself against her thighs. She was sobbing, her cheeks glistening with tears. Zarene had never seen her look so young. Her hand reached for Keyan's. It plopped to the ground, just short of her chhuba's sleeve.

'Keyan … this won't work.'

She went ignored.

'You seh-you said it's guh-good, honest work. That you make it quick and painless. It'll be the h-highest mercy. Please … please, don't punish your didi like this.'

A quiet, punctuated only by Keyan's hiccups and Zarene's laboured breaths, festered between them. Zarene almost dozed off again. Then, swiping the back of her hand across the underside of her nose, Keyan crawled closer. Zarene caught the flash of silver she tried to conceal behind the span of her chhuba.

'I don't know what else to do,' Keyan said, her bottom lip jutting out.

Creator, she is so young.

Summoning the last of her strength, Zarene propped herself on her elbow and threw her free arm around Keyan.

'Don't cry, little one.'

Keyan returned her hug. Winding her arms tightly around her torso, she lifted her to sit up. Zarene waited for the warmth she had come to expect from such affection, but found nothing but more shivers. She rested her cheek on Keyan's sinewy shoulder, and leant in as Keyan rocked her.

'I have never met another like you, Keyan. So sharp of mind, so brave, so proud, so noble.'

Keyan stilled their motion with a firm hand. Something shifted.

'I'm sorry I kept you from your family so long,' Zarene continued. 'I'm sorry I lied. I'm sorry I ever stopped my palanquin that day in the jungle. I'm sorry I let Dai Ma down … sorry for being so selfish. I'm sorry—'

There was a swift, sloppy crunch of bone. A jolt of pain exploded in her neck. Her mouth filled with the taste of iron. *What have I done?* She willed her hands to claw at Keyan's back for an anchor, but there was no feeling. Just what remained of her, floating and fading.

Her head fell forward. A wintry emptiness blackened her senses, and she slumped into oblivion.

NINE

Zarene batted her eyes open to a haze of yellow. Tightly tucked to her chest, her limbs reverberated with a strong, soothing heartbeat. She was warm. Snug as a swaddled baby. A rocking motion made her eyelids grow heavy. She wiggled her fingers and toes, savouring the return of sensation in them. Smiling, she buried her nose deeper between her knees and chest.

Blood rushed to her head. Her prickling feet sought grounding, but came up against a sticky barrier. Zarene pushed sideways with her elbow. It was a rubbery translucent skin, thin but unyielding. Starting to see stars, Zarene ducked her chin into her neck, rounded her shoulders and thrust her elbows and legs out.

A rip crackled down the length of her spine to her bare bottom. The foreign skin peeled off her, smarting like it did when she yanked bodily hairs off with sugar taffy. Freeing her nose and eyes, she realized she had been hanging upside down. She grabbed the clumps of peel just as her falling legs spun her upright.

The branch the skin hung from bobbed as she tried to claw her way up. She was at the top of a gargantuan chamber, roughly the shape of a dome. Trees with bright yellow leaves bordered it, covering its walls from floor to ceiling. Barring wayward branches at the very top, their growth had been restrained to the periphery with scaffolding-like contraptions.

The floor beneath was solid stone. A drop from where Zarene hung, naked as the day she was born, would most definitely break a bone or two. *No respite, even in death.* The scaffolding offered a safe way down, but there was still the length of the branch to cover.

Something brushed, then fluttered against the sensitive skin below her navel. Then against her shin and the crook of her neck. She flicked her head, but the ticklish feeling persisted. Zarene turned her head to see what it was, and screamed.

Dark eyes embedded in dark brown fur stared up at her. Bronze leaf-shaped antennas sprouted from the creature's head. Its prickly legs, kinked like a spider's, supported a plush body. Its ochre, paper-thin, almost frayed wings looked sprinkled with cinnamon, their tips dipped in cumin powder.

Moths. She was covered in them.

The suspended skin slipped from Zarene's grasp as she tried to shake them off. Her scream held, even after they cleared off. She landed on her back with a thud. Thankfully, there was no crunch. Rubbing her aching head as she sat up, her fingers slipped under her soft, clean tresses. They grazed a freshly healed scar at the base of her neck. She shuddered at the memory of the pain that had come with it. It had really happened. She really was dead.

Circular jute baskets were laid out across the floor, and a few hardy midsized cauldrons stood vigil over them. A coal brazier burnt near the centre of the chamber, even though the iridescent gold light streaming through some of the trees let on the day was still young.

Maybe the sun never set in the afterlife.

Next to the brazier, at the chamber's very centre, stood a stone-top table whose base was embedded into the floor. On it sat some neatly folded homespun fabric. Two sets of robes. Swatting the moths from her face, Zarene shook one loose and slipped her arms through it.

The mahagony-coloured garment was like a sleeveless qaba that touched the floor. Instead of an open front, it wrapped about the torso, and was cinched and bound at the waist by running a sash through slits in the fabric. Its bottom half flared out like a ghagra and, to Zarene's delight, possessed pockets on either side.

As she admired the fabric's smooth fall over her curves, she noticed an inscription peering out from underneath the second set of robes. It ran along the tabletop's border:

There is a song that they will not hear;

A strain so strange and yet so dear...

A low grunt echoed through the chamber. Zarene spun around, alarmed, and looked up. Tearing its way out from another skin, one barely discernable because of its yellow camouflage, came a fair and flat figure with razor straight hair.

'Keyan!'

Zarene grabbed the second robe and dashed towards Keyan with outstretched arms. Keyan did not require catching, though. She hauled herself up the skin, and walked the length of the branch with the agility of a cat. Hopping down, scaffold to scaffold, she met Zarene at the bottom with her arms defensively crossed over her breasts. The show of modesty drew Zarene's attention to a mottled red gash over her heart.

'Keyan,' Zarene gasped. Her mouth hung open.

Keyan snatched the robe from her and turned around to dress. She slapped a moth off her head. 'What is this place? Where are we?'

Zarene shook her head, questions and apologies lumped in her throat, and looked inside the baskets. They were compartmented, filled with webs. Slung amidst them were thumb-sized buds. Cocoons. A moth flew past her nose. Worms—fat, long and white—crawled the wall of yellow leaves.

'It's a silk farm,' Zarene said, lips cracking into a wide grin. The moths, devious as they looked, did not seem so bad now. 'It's the grove from my dreams.'

'Your dreams tell you what to do next?'

Keyan's hand was at her collar, clutching it shut to hide the scar. The strain of a lifetime of hardship and months on the road no longer marred her face. Her lashes were the same black as her hair, and her box lid lips shone a moist russet. The brown splotches on her skin had evened, leaving it the colour of turmeric-laced milk. There was a glow about her, like she had run up a hill and back down without shedding a drop of sweat.

'I don-I don't know,' Zarene said. 'The scion … she destroyed the ghagra. I swear.'

Keyan clicked her tongue and rolled her eyes. 'That's not why you had the dreams, though, yeah? So, why're we here, then?'

Zarene's eyes flickered to Keyan's heart. She bit the inside of her cheeks, then drew a sharp breath. 'We find her. We find the howr.'

The way out was inconspicuous. It was a thin lopsided sweep of an opening in a wall painted the same yellow as the leaves. The girls would likely not have noticed had it not been for the sparse line of moths streaming through it.

The crack opened out to a dark and narrow tunnel. A distant drone filled the darkness. Fires in sconces were fixed to the left-hand wall at long intervals. The ground was slippery and shone an inky black in the scant light, almost like water. There were steps leading down, some flat, some so steep the girls needed to jump.

The lower they descended, the hotter it got. The steady drone grew louder and louder, distinguishing itself as rapid, gushing water. Leading the way, Keyan came to an abrupt halt, and Zarene crashed into her.

Before them, the right wall gave out, exposing their path to a deep gorge. A powerful current of water streamed in down below from a slender waterway up ahead. It collected in a rock-studded pool so vast it did not seem to have a bank opposite to where they stood. Dangling over it like a full moon was a giant sphere constructed entirely of silk webs.

Zarene and Keyan pushed themselves up against the left wall and edged down till they arrived at the bottom of the gorge, almost level with the water. Zarene stared at the web structure as moths flicked themselves at it and swirled about it.

'What is it?'

'Best not to find out,' Keyan said, her hand reflexively grasping for her pipe. 'There's no telling how deep the water is, or what's hiding in it.'

Their path branched two ways: towards the rush of water and away from it. From the force with which the water entered, Keyan guessed it came from a waterfall, which meant a dead end and a certain second death. They turned on their heel and followed the stillness instead. The path led them to another tunnel over and away from the pool. Its incline spiralled round and round in the dark for what seemed like hours, perhaps even days. Zarene wondered if this was to be her sentence. If she had arrived in hell.

They turned another bend and recoiled. Sunlight, bright and blissful in all its glory, cascaded in through another thin, lopsided opening. They were hardly two steps out in the open when a shrill screech pierced the air and a mass of feathers with talons sharp as knives swooped down on them.

Zarene and Keyan dropped to the ground and peered up through parted fingers. A golden eagle circled above them, its wingspan roughly the length of four outstretched arms. Mostly brown, its neck was covered in dark golden feathers. White feathers made up the underside of its wings and tail. The girls pressed their heads to the ground as it dove towards them again. Large as a foal, it landed before them and appraised them with shrewd yellow eyes. When the girls braved to draw their palms from their eyes, it splayed its wings to bow. Then it launched itself into the sky once more, disappearing behind a faraway cluster of trees.

They were at the edge of a green valley. The mountain they had emerged from, along with a few others, formed a protective wall around it. Great hairy yaks, mountain ponies and goats grazed on and lounged about in the lush grass; geese honked and skittered about with protracted necks; and roosters and chickens surveyed the grounds for something to peck at.

A quaint, rectangular cottage of red and sandy yellow brick stood to one side. It was very tall for a simple cottage—two floors from the looks of it—and was fitted with high windows on each floor. Two-thirds of its length was covered by a sloped roof of terracotta shingles. The remaining third was flat-topped for an open terrace.

Too hesitant to knock, Zarene and Keyan strolled the cottage's flagstone patio. There was another grey structure behind the cottage. It had a raised porch at the front and a thatched roof.

Further behind, clothes swayed from lines suspended between poles. Keyan launched herself at them to gather a swath of olive in her arms. Her chhuba. Zarene's qaba, salwar, kameez, and underthings were hanging there as well, scrubbed of all blood.

Keyan clutched the chhuba to her chest and sniffed it. 'She washed them. Why would she wash our clothes?'

The clothes were still damp. Zarene let hers be and scanned the mountains for a way out. If they were dead, *was* there a way out? They took their time circling back to the cottage's front door. Standing there, unsure what to do next, they became acutely aware of the pangs of hunger gnawing inside them.

Zarene climbed the two steps to the door and raised her hand to knock, but froze.

Her world had been turned upside down, yet she still yearned—not so much to return to her old life as to master the craft that consumed her so completely. The thrill of every possibility waiting on the other side of the door raised gooseflesh across her skin. Despite everything, she couldn't—didn't want to—deny this part of who she was. And for that she was ashamed.

Lowering her hand, she drew away.

'Stop dawdling down there,' a woman called, making both of them jump out of their skin. 'The tea will stick to the pot!'

The impatient voice boomed through a window on the second floor. Zarene and Keyan deliberated with nervous but curious looks, and stepped through the unlocked door.

Keyan gasped. In a corner by the door, propped beside an assortment of footwear, a walking staff, a sheathed scimitar, a bow and a quiver of arrows was her pipe. It gleamed from a fresh polish. Snatching it up, she unclasped the spout and dabbed a finger on the blade. Still sharp.

The cottage's interior was larger, much larger, than its outer façade let on. Its lay resembled that of a high-ceilinged courtyard. The ground floor comprised a large open space. An intricately crafted rug lay on the sandstone floor, stacked with cushions. The high windows on the far side bracketed a rustic but downy divan between them, and tapestries of rich embroidery adorned the walls. Folding tables for individual use were neatly stacked to one side.

A wall to their right separated the sitting area from the kitchen. A staircase without rails protruded from the left-hand wall. It curved up to a gallery that spanned three sides. Each of the roof's slopes was fixed with a sunroof, permitting plenty of natural light onto both floors.

'The cups are on the second shelf,' the woman's voice called from upstairs. 'There's a basket of nokshi pithas in the dry store, if you like.'

Crispy fried rice cakes dunked in syrup. Their stomachs growled in unison.

In the kitchen, a rounded pot with a pouring spout sat atop the mud stove. The tea simmering within was thick and light brown from a generous helping of milk. Upon locating the basket, Keyan shoved an entire pitha into her mouth and groaned in bliss.

'Here,' she said, holding one out to Zarene. 'I'd not thought it possible, but they're even better than the ones you'd had at the mela.'

'What are you doing?' Zarene hissed. 'You can't just go around eating strange people's food!'

'Well, why not? We're not going to die, yeah?'

Keyan's collar fell slack as she busied her hands. Zarene's chest tightened at the sight of the angry scar peeking out from underneath.

'You have your pipe now,' Zarene said. 'We can just collect our clothes and be on our way.'

'Our way where? You're dead and so am I, I'm sure of it. It's not like I can ever forget. Now, if you're still too gutless to face the howr woman, then I'm never talking to you again, yeah? And by the looks of this place, you're not going to like that one bit.'

Zarene huffed in surrender. She took out three earthen cups from a wobbly cabinet and nestled them in the pitha basket. Then she searched for a thick rag to handle the pot with.

Keyan led the way upstairs, her pipe uncapped and ready to strike. Balancing the basket in one hand and the teapot in the other, Zarene followed Keyan around the gallery to an open door right above the main entrance downstairs.

A regal bed, bathed in beams of clear sunlight, came into view as they approached the threshold. It was the longest bed Zarene had ever laid eyes on. Wrought of braided wood, it created the illusion that it had been grown from the parquet. The edges of its headboard were etched with floral motifs, and a vignette protruded from its smooth surface.

Amidst the fluffed pillows and lush emerald quilt of leaf-shaped cutwork and velvety applique lay an uncommonly large woman. A sleek, voluminous cloud of midnight violet hair splayed out about her head and shoulders. Her transluscent, wheat-toned arms lay long and sinewy at her sides over the quilt. Her skin was flushed pink like Keyan's, but was covered in a thin layer of sweat.

'Ah, good,' she sighed in relief. 'We were beginning to have second thoughts about putting our faith in you. Come in, come in.'

She sat up with effort. The quilt dropped from her chest, baring the silver satin slip she had on.

The girls stood stock-still at the room's threshold. Something was wrong with her face. It could have been the bright light playing tricks on them. Perhaps she was too beautiful to comprehend. But to Zarene, it looked like her features were in flux, and painfully so.

'Well, don't just stand there. Our blood is running cold. Pour us the tea.'

As Zarene set the basket and teapot on the floor, she noticed the muslin orna draped over an airing rack to the side of the room. She poured out a cup and gave it to the howr, snatching her hand away as soon as she could.

'It's all sticky,' the howr said. Her lips curved in a grimace before quivering, stretching and skewing. 'Next time, use a tray.'

She took a sip of the tea, sighed in relief, and leant back against the headboard. Her wriggling features steadied somewhat: an arrowhead nose, high, rounded cheekbones, feline blue eyes and doughy, bow-shaped lips that shone like wine. Closing her eyes, she smiled.

'Go on, pour yourselves a cup. Have a seat.'

Zarene and Keyan continued to stare at her.

The vignette carved on the headboard had a tree with weeping leaves running through the centre. Curved in the shape of a wave, it stood beside a cliff. A throng of women gathered at its edge to watch one of their own climb down the weeping leaves to get to the barren lands below.

Sensing Keyan's fingers flex against her pipe, Zarene cleared her throat.

'Um, Sahiba? Are we … is this what comes after?'

Eyes still shut, the howr took another sip of tea and shook her head.

'So, we're not dead?'

'No,' the howr said. 'You will likely live longer than what is expected of your kind.'

'But we did die.'

'That you did. The both of you. But we brought you here and gave each of you one of our own lives. And now you wish to repay our kindness by killing us.' Opening her eyes, she fixed a pointed look behind Zarene, on Keyan. 'Put that blade away, Khyana Sresht. Your anger is misguided and you do not want the burden of taking all the lives I have remaining.'

'My Baa'd gone mad because of you,' Keyan seethed.

'Your father and his patron wished to lay claim on us, defile us, and humiliate us. You should be no angrier at us than you would be at deer being hunted for sport.'

'Yeah? If you're so innocent, why'd you not meet us earlier? Why'd you get our men—good, honourable men—killed like that? Why'd you leave us in the middle of the bloody Heemdangas without any warm clothes or food? Answer me that, then.'

'You should know, Khyana Sresht, that we had not intended on parting with two of our lives in such quick succession. That taking Zarene Maimoona's life would cause you such distress was unprecedented. But also know that we would not have granted you our life if we didn't consider you worthy.

'The mortal body can only accommodate one life force at a time. The old life must be drained for the metamorphosis to work. Now, the essence of your person can only be preserved if the soul is kept intact. Had there been any final rites performed on your corpse—'

'Our souls would have been freed from our bodies,' Zarene said, shuddering. 'That's why you brought us all the way out here.'

'Precisely. And to test your commitment, of course.'

'Commi—' Zarene's head spun. 'This is hardly what I wanted. I never wanted to be anything besides myself! And I'd made my decision! I saw that I was wrong, and I decided to destroy the ghagra, and I decided to go home!'

'Tsk, tsk, tsk,' the howr said, clamping her eyes shut in irritation. 'You are too old to be presuming the river will bend to your every will. Besides, you wished for the ability to replicate the ghagra. Now you have the blood to do it.'

Zarene's heart leapt into her throat. She rifled through her mind for the secret she did not have before, but came up short. 'No. I still have no idea how it's made.'

'No. We have but given you the gift, and gifts rarely amount to much if one lacks the proper training.'

'How long will that take? To learn, I mean.'

'How long will it take you to master your jealousy?'

Zarene drew a sharp breath. The howr tipped her head back to empty her cup.

'Don't go answering questions with questions,' Keyan snapped, stamping her pipe on the floor. 'Are you going to teach her, yes or no?'

'Is that not what we are saying?'

'Again with the questions!' Keyan drew the pipe back to strike.

'Keyan!' Shoving the pipe away, Zarene inserted herself between Keyan and the bed. To the howr she said, 'She's right, though. We need answers. If you wish to teach me, then why not just teach me? Why give us a life we didn't ask for?'

A melodic sigh spilt from the howr's morphing bow-shaped lips. 'Because we're tired. Of living, that is. We've roamed these forsaken lands for eight hundred long years, been hunted, paraded like cattle, worshipped, enslaved, murdered. We arrived here with ninety-nine lives, and are now left with only a handful more. We could have ended it quickly, once and for all, but to waste abilities like ours is folly. Which is why we decided to impart them to those we could put our faith in.'

She had faith in Zarene, this stranger she barely knew. Something about that made Zarene's insides bloom with warmth. But there was also doubt and fear. How could she trust such a creature?

'And now that you've accomplished that … given us your life, I mean … if we wanted to go—?'

'We wouldn't stop you. But there will be no returning and our tutelage will be lost to you forever.'

'Oh.' Zarene's knees grew unsteady. 'Then, I don't know. I'll need some time to think it through.'

'No,' Keyan said. She placed a firm hand on Zarene's arm. 'We're staying.'

Zarene whipped her head around to look at Keyan. Keyan tipped her head in a slight nod. The decision was final.

'But I'll need to send word home to Shandrabad. As does Keyan to her family.'

'Indeed, you must,' the howr said. 'You may use Garu for that. But all correspondences must go through us. We will not tolerate the secret of our abode being divulged to mortals.'

'I'm sorry, what's a Garu?'

'Our most loyal eagle companion, yes. He has been caring for us these past few days. We told him he could go hunt once you two finished your metamorphoses.' Her eyes bubbled under her lids. She held out the teacup. 'Now, pour us another cup and leave us to rest. We cannot do much till we've regained our strength. We'll be in need of meat. As will you. Best get dinner started, hmm?'

Zarene refilled her cup and offered her a pitha before turning to leave. At the door, she spun around, splashing tea from the pot everywhere.

'Forgive me, but what do we call you?'

The howr emptied her cup in one gulp and slid back under the quilt.

'We do not recall the name given us by Creator, but we gave ourselves the good name, Firuzah.'

Downstairs, Zarene and Keyan munched on enough pithas to placate their stomachs till dinner. The yak's milk in the tea was too thick for Zarene's liking, so she let Keyan finish the rest of the pot. She then went to the kitchen to take stock of what they had to work with. She was in the process of clumsily peeling a few onions and mincing some garlic and ginger when Keyan returned holding a clucking chicken.

'I can't eat it if I kill it,' Keyan explained in response to Zarene's quizzical look.

Zarene had always considered it odd when Keyan ate meat on the road. To the best of her knowledge, Qokhurans and other believers of the All Knowing were usually vegetarian. It made sense now, considering Keyan was never responsible for preparing their food, but it still rang strange given what she did to earn her livelihood. What she had done at Zarene's behest.

It didn't matter, though. Zarene was ready to cook Keyan's meals till the end of time. She grabbed and chopped off the chicken's head without a moment's hesitation. Delegating dicing duties to Keyan, she settled down on the kitchen doorstep to pluck the chicken of its feathers.

She'd barely cleared the neck when Keyan joined her. A soft breeze scattered the plucked feathers across the flagstone. Hunkering down, Keyan collected them in a pail. The sight flooded Zarene with a fresh surge of guilt.

'Why'd you do it, little one? You would have made it to the pass. You would have made it home.'

Keyan's shoulders grew rigid and her box-lid lips contracted. 'I couldn't, though, could I? I was so busy being angry about Baa, I'd not seen you slipping away just like him. Not until it was too late.'

'I meant all those things I said. You know, when ...' Zarene stopped herself from grazing the scar on her neck. 'You're a noble friend, and you've given me more than I can ever hope to return. But I am where I'm meant to be now. You don't need to waste your time by my side anymore.'

'Let me decide that for myself, yeah?'

Sighing, Zarene looked up at the sight before them. If what Firuzah said was true—although Zarene didn't trust the howr all that much—she had time to pay Keyan back, time to atone for every ill she'd ever committed. But first, she would answer her heart's call. If she didn't, it would have all been for nothing.

The grasslands darkened under the growing shadow of the mountain. Overhead, the line between rock and sky blurred as white clouds drifted over snowy peaks. A streak of marigold cut through it all. Its deepening colour, from red to purple to indigo, slowly engulfed the white. When all turned dark, the white would return, luminescent in starlight.

Zarene envisioned a ghagra that could depict such minute changes in the sky. She no longer wondered who'd make such a thing. Now, it was only a matter of how and when.

But first dinner. All good things began on a full stomach.

ABOUT THE AUTHOR

Anjum N. Choudhury had a nomadic childhood, moving between Dhaka, Kathmandu, New Delhi and the Hague. Fiction was one of the few constants in her life, eventually evolving into a creative outlet. *The Divining Thread* is her first published novella. It started out as a short story that was rejected by every fantasy magazine she'd submitted it to, which in hindsight turned out to be for the best.

Anjum became a policy researcher after earning a B.A. in Economics and Mathematics from Mount Holyoke College. Currently based in Dhaka, Bangladesh, she is getting her M. Sc. in Global Public Policy with a special focus on Climate Policy from SOAS University of London.

ABOUT THE AUTHOR